LA SAGOUINE

Also by Antonine Maillet
in English translation

Fiction
The Tale of Don l'Orignal (translated by Barbara Godard)
Pélagie: The Return to Acadie (translated by Philip Stratford)
Mariaagélas: Maria, Daughter of Gélas
(translated by Ben-Z. Shek)
The Devil Is Loose (translated by Philip Stratford)
On the Eighth Day (translated by Wayne Grady)

Drama
La Sagouine (translated by Luis de Céspedes)
Evangeline the Second (translated by Luis de Céspedes)
Gapi and Sullivan (translated by Luis de Céspedes)

Children's Literature
Christopher Cartier of Hazelnut,
Also Known as Bear (translated by Wayne Grady)

La Sagouine

ANTONINE MAILLET

Translated by Wayne Grady

Cover photo of Viola Léger by Paul McCarthy, courtesy Le Pays de la Sagouine.
Cover photo of bucket, istockphoto.com
Cover and book design by Julie Scriver.
Printed in Canada
10 9 8 7 6 5 4 3 2

Library and Archives Canada Cataloguing in Publication

Maillet, Antonine, 1929-
[Sagouine. English]
La Sagouine / Antonine Maillet; translated by Wayne Grady.
Translation of the French play of the same title.
ISBN 978-0-86492-415-5
I. Grady, Wayne II. Title. III. Title: Sagouine. English.
PS8526.A4S413 2007   C842'.54   C2007-904317-8

Goose Lane Editions acknowledges the generous support of the Canada Council
for the Arts, the Government of Canada through the Canada Book Fund (CBF),
and the Government of New Brunswick through the Department of Culture, Tourism,
and Healthy Living.

Goose Lane Editions
500 Beaverbrook Court, Suite 330
Fredericton, New Brunswick
CANADA E3B 5X4
www.gooselane.com

For my brother Achille

Contents

Preface

This is a true story I'm about to tell you. The story of La Sagouine, a woman of the sea, born with the century and practically with her feet in water. And water was her fortune: she was the daughter of a cod fisherman, went out with sailors, became the wife of a caplin and oyster fisherman. And worked as a scrubwoman, too, making her living kneeling by her pail with her hands in water.

That's how I found her, down there with her mop and her rags, hunched over her dirty pail that for a half-century had been gathering up all the dirt of the country. Troubled water it was, but still capable of reflecting the face of this woman who has never seen herself mirrored in anything but the dirt of others.

I give her to you just as I found her. I haven't touched her up. I've left her with her wrinkles and cracks and with her language intact. She doesn't speak joual or chiac or international French. She speaks the common language of her father and grandfathers, handed down straight from the sixteenth century. She's not aware that she's her own dictionary, her own race, her own flip side of the coin. She defines herself as a "citizen apart from the whole." What she doesn't know is that the part belonging to others is more whole than her own.

She's seventy-two years old. She has fight in her yet. She is alone. Her only worldly possessions are her pail, her mop and her rags. Her public is before her and around her, but mostly at her feet, in her pail. When she talks, it's to her pail of troubled water. That's what she was doing when I heard her.

A.M.
Montreal, January 7, 1971

La Sagouine

On Work

So maybe I do have a bit of dirt on my face and my skin's all cracked, but at least my hands are clean! They ought to be, I've had them in water long enough. I spent my whole life cleaning. That don't mean I'm soft in the head, you know. I clean other people's houses. No wonder I look dirty. People like us spend all our time taking dirt off other people, rubbing and scrubbing and scraping up wads of gum so they can have a nice place to live in. Not us, of course, no one comes to clean our places for us.

You won't catch them coming to wash our clothes, nor sew them nor mend them neither. No wonder they think we're soft in the head — we're wearing all their old hand-me-down coats and stuff, for the love of Christ. I suppose we should be grateful they still got some religion into them, at least it makes them think of us from time to time when they got some old junk they want to get rid of. Charity, they calls it. Their old junk and their old clothes that was new once, like we never dream of having something new once in a while. We get all their old hand-me-downs as payment for the work we do for them, but of course by then they're hardly the stuff of dreams, if you catch my drift. You see a woman wearing a velvet hat for ten years, and at first you think it looks pretty good and you wouldn't mind wearing it yourself, but then after a while it starts to look kind of beat up and pretty soon it's like someone stuck an old buckwheat pancake on her head, and of course that's when they give it to you. And their old shawls when no one wears shawls any more, and lace-up boots when everyone's wearing shoes. Sometimes you even get two boots for the same foot, or a coat that's too tight to button up, which don't matter much because they already cut all the buttons off of it anyways. Oh yeah, they could say we don't dress too good.

Not good enough to go to church, that's for sure. People like to get dressed up for church. At least when they go to church on Sunday. Me, I don't have any nice clothes, which is why I only go to church on weekdays, when I go at all. There's lots of us don't go at all any more, because the priest, he told us that going to mass on a weekday don't count. All we're doing is adding on another sin if we go to mass on Friday when we still have Sunday mass on our conscience. Anyways, when Gapi heard that he stopped going to mass altogether, Fridays or Sundays, so I don't get to church much myself these days.

Couldn't get to church on St. Blaise's Day, for example, to get my throat blessed, because I had to do their houses for them that morning while they went. And so I had tonsillitis all year, also the mumps. Them as got their throats blessed like they wanted, well, you should see them strutting around and looking down their noses at the rest of us with our fevers and such. Yeah, well, fevers, they're like any other disease — they're not for everyone, just for the select few, the same ones who keep catching them over and over. Funny, ain't it, that we're always the last to get whatever's going around except when it comes to fevers and lice? Yeah, well.

They don't want our kids sitting up at the front of the class with their own kids; they say our kids have head lice. They never had head lice themselves, of course, and they're more afraid of a few lice and fleas than they are of catching cancer. They must think lice and fleas can swallow a person whole. They can put a pound of shoe polish and bear grease in their own hairdos, but let them see a louse the size of a fish egg on somebody else's head and it's Oh my God, don't let that kid sit next to mine! Send him to the back of the class where he can't see or hear nothing. It's no picnic trying to learn something when you can't see the blackboard or hear the teacher.

And it's no picnic learning to speak proper and carry yourself like everyone else when they won't even let you say something to them without treating you like an uppity hick from the back of beyond, either. Go on, try saying, How's it going, eh? to Dominique's wife the next time you pass her when you're going in her front door on your way to washing her floors. Watch her turn up her nose like your words was something smelly the cat dragged in. So the next time, you go in through the back door and you keep your trap shut.

I wouldn't know what to say to them anyways. Oh, they can talk up a storm amongst themselves about their family or their trips overseas or their summer houses and their winter houses and their kids going off to college or the government. What would we say to that? We don't have any kids in college or relatives in the States, we don't go moving into different houses every time the weather changes or hopping from one country to another like a bunch of gadabouts. We don't take vacations because we don't have jobs. We work in their houses, and it's not like they give you paid vacations or anything. Or forty-hour workweeks, or old-age pensions. You spend your old age like you spent your youth, scrubbing and cleaning . . . Yeah, well.

Not that it wouldn't be good to be able to take it easy, too, in our old age, our feet planted in good soil and a few nice things around us. After the lean years come the years of plenty, or so they says. No, I'm not talking about traipsing around in trailers with a bunch of other golden-agers, I'm not asking for the moon here. There's some of them spend their declining years like that, it seems, travelling from town to town and from one country to the next in them big trailers, they look more like houses than houses do, from what I've heard. Anyone who can afford a house on wheels like that, that they can pull down the road in their old age, I imagine they must have owned their own house with a full basement and everything when they was young.

But what Gapi's never been able to get, he says, is why anyone would want to pull up and traipse about like that when they got everything they need right here at home? You got your three square meals a day at your own table; you get a better night's sleep on your own spring mattress; every fall you get to change out of your summer underwear into your winter long johns; you got your front porch with your rocker on it that you can rock back as far as you want so you can see everything around you and out over the bay, too . . . Well, it don't take much to make him happy, is all I can say.

What I say to him is, maybe when a person has her fill of all of that luxury and has seen far enough ahead of herself, when she gets to a certain age, maybe she can't help wanting to see more, to see further than the bay, and maybe that's when she signs up for the Golden Age Club and takes to the road.

Me, I don't know, I don't see the harm if we went somewhere, you know, just up and went, just to see what it's like, poke our noses in here and there, with nothing else to worry about. Seems to me it could be fun seeing something you never seen before, like the falls at Niagara Falls, maybe, or maybe that soldier fella in the plaid skirt that plays the bagpipes down in Nova Scotia. I wouldn't mind seeing that some day, not for any good reason, just to see it.

And while we're at it I wouldn't mind dropping in to the old family farm on Prince Edward Island, too, see if it's changed at all in the past hundred years. Not to stay, of course, I wouldn't want to move back there or anything. Just to see what the country's like, and the people. I'd like to see if it's true that the gardens come up sooner there than they do here, maybe drop in on some of the relatives who've been there since after the Expulsion. They say that in the old country you don't need to tell anyone your name, they can tell a Thibodeau by his eyes, or a Leblanc by his nose, or a Bourgeois by the cleft in his chin, or a Goguen by the way he chokes on his "r"s like someone rammed an orange down in his throat.

Oh yeah, there's plenty of people from around here who have relatives down there. It'd be good to get them all together some-day, let everyone get to know each other, be able to pat some old guy on the back and call him by his first name. You see a descendant of one of your own ancestors and you say, Hi, there, Pit-à-Boy-à-Thomas-à-Picoté, how's it going, eh? Then you see someone across the room looks just like you do, and who's speaking like it's you who's talking, and who has the same job as you, and who wouldn't look down her nose at you just because you're a cleaning lady who's never done nothing much and never been nowhere.

Anyways, we never see nothing but other people's houses when we go in to clean them every day the Good Lord gives us. Where we get down on their hardwood floors and their flowered linoleum like we're going to pray. Except you don't pray, you scrub. You scrub and pick up the dirt and bring it home with you in your pail. All that dirt belonging to someone else in the bottom of your bucket . . . Yeah, well, anyways . . .

This here, now, this is the dirtiest place I ever cleaned, I'll tell you that for nothing. They even got gum stuck on the floor, as if there's any need for that. Holy Mother of Christ, some people have no pride into them at all! Give La Sagouine some new li-noleum like this and she'd put her gum in the spittoon where it belongs, right there with her tobacco juice. Everything in its proper place, that's what I say, and a proper place for everything. Of course they don't have no spittoon here, they don't think it's the height of fashion no more. So that means they got gum stuck everywhere, and cigarette ashes all over the place. On the tables, on the arms of the chairs, on the rug, in those little ashtrays no bigger than my belly button they got scattered about the house. Put a nice big spittoon in the middle of the room and you'd save a lot of sweeping up ashes and scraping up gum everywhere.

They think they don't make much of a mess because they smoke with their lips all puckered up — like this — and don't even mention chewing tobacco, you'll have them feeding the gulls for sure. At least with chewing tobacco maybe you spit more, but there's a lot less smoke. And it ain't spit that dirties up a place, it's smoke. You can't shovel smoke into a spittoon, can you? Me, it makes me sick to my stomach to think every time I take a breath I'm breathing in smoke that's already been in someone else.

And they get sick, too, some of them, even with all their beautified skin and their hair all curled on the top of their heads and their fingernails as long and pointed as a church steeple, smelling enough of deodorant and toothpaste to knock you off your feet. Oh, they look pretty clean from the outside. But what about the inside, eh? A person never knows what's crawling around inside of him unless they go in and take a look. Oh, yeah, I know: they can operate now and go in and see what's in there. Open chest, open heart, open noggin . . . yeah, they can even open up your skull these days and take a look at your brains! They can split your head open right down to your shoulders, from what I hear.

You won't catch La Sagouine lying in no operating room getting her body opened up to see what's in her head, no way. Anyways, whatever she's got in there she's never kept hidden from anyone. Gapi, now, he says that if we could get a look at what doctors are finding in people's guts these days it wouldn't all be turkey dinners, that's for sure . . . I wouldn't know about that.

Seems to me that one cut-open body would look pretty much like any other cut-open body. It's only when you close them up again and sew their skin up around their necks and across their bellies that a rich person's body stops looking like a poor person's. Anyway, rich people get sick mostly on account of their nerves, and sick nerves don't usually show. They might break out in little fits from time to time, but you don't get your skin going all black, or your face breaking out in boils, or your joints aching, or crossed eyes and water on the knee, which is what you get from cleaning. That's what makes a body look all wonky like. Those fits, though, all the rich get them, but they cover them up with nice clothes and nobody notices. That's what I tell Gapi: there's rich sick and there's poor sick and it's not the same sickness. Each to his own gout, as they say . . .

It ain't easy being poor. Some people think it's only the rich that has troubles. But when the rich get trouble it's only in their hearts or their heads. We get our trouble in our bones. Yeah . . . there comes a time when there's nothing much left of a person but their bones, and that's when it's not so good to have all your troubles in your bones. The doctors call it rheumatics or arthuritis or whatever. Being doctors, they got to call it something. And they give you little bottles of liniament to rub on yourself. But you can rub your skin all you want with every kind of liniament in the almanac and it won't make a blind bit of difference to the pain in your bones. Too much cold stored up in them, too much lumbago and shingles. When you spend your whole life scrubbing and bent double over a floor, you can rub your bones with liniament till you're blue in the face and you'll just end up bent over triple, or quadruple. It's not that easy to straighten up when you're poor. The poor never got used to walking around with their heads held high when they were young.

Not when they were young, and not when they're old, neither. Poor people were meant to drag their feet from street to street and door to door . . . dragging their boots and their rags and their buckets. You take your boots off at the door so you don't get the floor dirty you came to wash; you bring your own mop and pail and soap; you kneel down on an old piece of cardboard so as not to get your knees too wet; you take big swipes of floor to show them you ain't afraid of hard work; you scrape up their gum with a knife and then polish the floor till the nail heads shine; you scrub and scrape and wash and rinse and wash again . . . and then, when you're done all that, they hand you your pay and a few old clothes they don't want to wear no more, and you go home with your skin a little more cracked and your bones aching a little more. But your hands are clean. Yes sir!

Damned right they are! These rich women can bathe in buttermilk and toilet water like there's no tomorrow, there won't never be one of them cleaner than La Sagouine, who's spent her whole life up to her elbows in water.

On Youth

Oh yeah, I was young once. That was when I was in my youth. Not just young like everybody else, but young and pretty, which is what counted. I used to look at myself in the mirror sometimes, yeah, I had a mirror in them days, and I didn't think I was all that hard to look at. No sir, I wasn't too hard to look at at all in them days, if I do say so myself. But them days are gone, just like you all'll be gone one day, too. But when them days was still here, when I was in my prime, well, they was the best of days. Yes they was, the very best of days.

Young kids today, they don't know that. They moan and they groan and they get on everyone's nerves. They don't know what they want. We knew what we wanted, all right. We knew exactly what it was we wanted. Not hard to figure out: we wanted everything. We maybe knew we couldn't have everything, but we wanted as much of it as we could get our hands onto. We weren't going to settle for half of nothing, no sirree bob! Not half a pancake, not half a house, and not half a man, neither. No, it's no time for halves when you're young. It's the time for big ideals, like the priests say, and Lord knows I had my share of them, big ideals I mean.

I was young and I had a pretty good figure. I still had all my teeth and all my hair. My skin was soft, too, and I used to file my nails to a point. It didn't hurt the eyes to look at me. And when I had that all figured out, I didn't have to rack my brains trying to find my ideals. Ideals are something that just comes to you by themselves, like. You lean against a telephone pole up by the Irving station or down at the dock, and for sure ideals'll come charging up from all over, each one as ideal as the next. All you got to do is pick the one you like. You might like them all, of course, but you can't have them all, not all at once, anyways. It's like Dominique's wife says about their son, he can't be a priest and a doctor and a lawyer all at the same time. But choosing one is hard, which is why he ended up in politics. Me, now, can you see me getting mixed up in politics? Eh? Me being a woman and all, and a woman from the boonies on top of that? No, a woman from the boonies pretty much has only the one choice. But when she makes it, she has to go all the way with it. She don't do nothing by halves. Because we all have our ideals, like I said. We don't have jobs, but we have ideals. A woman from the sticks who still has her looks and a bit of weight on her, who's taken good care of herself, she can still make her choice if she has any kind of head on her shoulders. One choice at a time, anyways.

So you lean up against a telephone pole, or you walk up and down Main Street from the mill end to the river end. And you wait. And you don't get too discouraged because it ain't long before your waiting's done, and then it's all them others who are waiting on you. Course you don't let on that you see them. You just go on chewing your gum and watching the river flowing under the bridge. You see them out the corner of your eye, though. You see every Tom, Dick and Harry puffing themselves up and running their hands through their hair, and the widow's boy hiding behind the porch swing, and big Pacifique himself poking his head out from behind the curtains. Ha! You ain't so foolish as to get yourself caught behind the curtains, though. Sagouine or no Sagouine, you've got your self-respect!

Still, you can't let self-respect get in the way of living for too long. Sometimes you got to change your ideals to suit the situation. You stick another piece of gum in your mouth, put a dab of perfume on your throat and behind your ears, and you dodge on up to the spring, where there's sure to be a crowd, always is. Except wherever there's a crowd that's where the Twin'll be, of course. And if you carry on out to the point, you'll find the Saint. Now there's a piece of work, that one! She'd charm the eyes off a snake with her rosaries and her religious medals. She took Basil-à-Pierre to all thirty-three Stations of the Cross, she did, and what they got up to between Stations is not for me to say . . . Anyways, we got schooners and steamships coming in here all the time. It's like I always say, as long as there's a dock somewhere . . . The sea, though, that's what saved us. Don't know where we'd be without caplin or clams or oysters. Not to mention sailors . . .

Oh yeah, we got them coming from all over, sailors. Often-times I couldn't understand a word came out of their mouths. Not exactly locals, if you know what I mean, but good people all the same. Gapi, now, he always said you had to keep an eye on them, but he never did trust anyone as far as he could throw them. Anyways, when the war got itself declared, the last one, there was this big steamship didn't see the war coming and didn't have time to clear the harbour. Had a load of Germans onto it, and the Germans weren't on our side. Well, they grabbed these Germans and threw them in jail, and there was them as said that was a good thing, that we couldn't have the enemy running around loose, attacking everyone. Well, stands to reason you can't have the wrong side running around attacking people. But how do you know what side's the right side? Then again, are all the good people on the same side? Don't seem hardly likely, does it? Makes it kind of hard to go to sleep at night, lying on your right side, and thinking you might've known a sailor or two in your day who seemed nice enough at the time but was on the wrong side all along.

I remember one of them who learned to mangle a few words

of English, although he wasn't from England or the States because it was obvious English wasn't exactly his mother tongue. No, he spoke some foreign language that didn't sound like anything. But he must've been to England or somewhere because he'd picked up a bit of English, and we eventually got so we could say a few words to each other. We're not used to talking much with outsiders, you know, and so we have a hard time making ourselves understood. But anyways, this fella . . .

He had yellow hair and troubled eyes, and it took me a while to find out why that was. His eyes, I mean, not his hair. In fact I don't think I ever did know the whole story. I had to piece it together from a few hints here and there about something bad that went on back in his country, wherever that was. He kept singing this same song over and over, something about a family being picked up and sent somewhere, at least that's what he told me it was about. He never laughed, that one, didn't seem to get much pleasure out of life like the rest of them did. That was why no one seemed to want to have him around, not even the girls from Butte-du-Moulin. But I didn't mind him that much.

At first I just sort of felt sorry for him, pitied him, like. He was so skinny, always sitting by himself up in the bow of the boat, singing that song. So eventually I just went up and sat down beside him. Never said boo, just looked out over the sea, him and me together like that. After a while he went back to his singing with me there, looking at me, and pretty soon we were speaking something that might be called English if you never heard it spoke before. Anyways, that's when I began noticing his eyes, and the trouble in them, and his big mop of yellow hair, and his hands, my God, he had hands on him that were cleaner and better cared for than a lawyer's, you should've seen them. And when he sang it made my insides churn like someone had punched me in the stomach. I don't know why that was, but it stopped me from wanting to go out with anyone else. I turned down a lot of good offers, too. Even Gapi noticed it.

It's hard. Hard to explain. It's like the sea had suddenly changed colour, like it was bluer than it used to be, and the fish had started swimming just below the surface so they could play with the gulls. The others tried to break us up and started calling us names, but I never paid no attention to them, well, hardly any . . .

Then one day war got declared. First light. Stopped the steamer at the entrance to the bay and threw all the sailors in jail for the duration, is what they said. For being on the wrong side. That's why it was all right to shoot them and throw them in prison. That's the day the sea changed colour all of a sudden and even the gulls didn't sound like their old selves anymore. A person could hardly go to sleep at night, couldn't settle down, just kept tossing and turning, trying to figure things out.

There comes a time when you stew over stuff like that more, because you're not as young as you used to be. That's what comes of getting old, I guess, thinking about things. Maybe it's because when you get old you have more time to think . . . hard to say. Gapi says thinking don't put nothing in your stomach but ulcers. Well, if that's so, Gapi must have a cast-iron stomach, because he hasn't done nothing but think his whole life, apart from grumble.

Oh, he's a grumbler, all right. It's his only fault. Used to come over him every time I went into the city. Wasn't used to being left by himself. In the old days I never had to travel far to make a living. I could get enough work right here at home, between the creek and the mill race, as you might say. However, you start getting on and you find yourself having to do things different. You realize you're not the only one out there trying to make ends meet. When you ain't exactly a spring chicken any more, you find there are lots out there who are younger than you. And you can do what you like, stick three pieces of gum in your mouth if you want to, and wear the cobblestones on Main Street down to little pebbles, but you won't catch a glimpse of Tom or Dick or Harry, or see big Pacifique's shadow in the curtains. So then you got to widen your search. Once a week you hop on the bus and get off in the city. Gapi, he could never swallow doing that. At least here he knew what was what. But in the city . . . Come with me, I told him, see for yourself. Nope. He grumbles but he don't budge. Not one for making things easy, is old Gapi.

Well, then the kids start growing up. I guess they got to sometime, can't be helped. It's just that once they get to a certain age they got eyes on them like hawks and they don't miss a thing, and they start asking questions. Like, why do you go into the city? How come if you're washing the bus station floor you don't take your mop and pail with you? So you take your mop and pail, because sooner or later you do end up washing the bus station floor. Then, when you're finished that, you do the floor of the church. Then you do CBAF, the radio station. And when you're down on all fours there in the CBC building, well, you can't get much lower than that. Because when you're bent over a wet floor with your hands in your bucket and your nose in your washrag you see faces coming up at you like from a mirror, faces that you know . . . Oh, yeah . . . A lot of people go through those buildings in the course of a day, and there's always one or two you know from back home on Main Street. They don't recognize you, of course, but you know who they are. And you begin to ask yourself when it was you sank lower than them, eh? On your knees beside your bucket or, well . . . everyone's got to get by, that's the it of it. That's what counts. Ideals or no ideals, there comes a time when a person has to live and make ends meet.

So long as you don't catch nothing else between the two ends. That's the biggest problem. You can get used to anything else, given enough time: being taken on, then let go, then taken back

26

on, then let go again, and all the while you know you're losing your spot at the telephone pole and ending up on the floor of the bus station. You can accept that, it goes with the territory. But why do you have to put up with all the rest of it? You remember Adelaide, Philip's daughter, P'tit Jean's granddaughter? If ever a beautiful creature walked the face of the earth in these parts, it was her. All plump and red and sly as a fox, that one. A right holy terror with the men, she was, they used to say it was in her blood. She wasn't a Boisfranc from Memramcook for nothing. Well, you know what happened to her, don't you? She wasn't three years at the pole before her legs was all swole up like molasses barrels, and boils come out all over her arms and face. Couldn't look at her after only three years, poor thing. If you think that's fair you got another think coming. Gapi, he says she let the horse into her own corn, but he don't know what he's talking about half the time. He just likes to grumble.

The worst was when a big ship'd come in from one of the old countries, and you thought for sure there'd be no shortage of work, but then you'd know the younger girls would be coming down from every hill around like a plague of grasshoppers on Egypt. Pour in from the furthest barnyards, worse than flies to honey. Fill the place up, they didn't care. Didn't matter if you were out at six o'clock when they were in town, all the telephone poles would be taken, the poles and the bridge. They'd even hang around on the church steps, if you can imagine! That was no way to behave, that bunch, they should've shown some respect. It was ignorant, that's what it was, coming in here and taking all our best spots. And you should've seen them, flour on their faces and beet juice on their cheeks! If anyone knew about flour and beet juice it was us, there wasn't much they could teach us about that. It made them look like I don't know what, and there they were taking the bread out of our mouths. And they wouldn't chew just any old gum, of course, like spruce gum, oh no, they had to be able to blow bubbles with it so they could pop them in our faces, just to show off! Well, before too long we'd had it up to here with their bubblegum and their puckered lips and their noses covered with flour. And all of them fatter than a channel marker on top of it all. Double-yolkers, we used to call them, because they all had one yolk too many, and they took it all away from us: our poles, our Main Street, our bread and butter. That's when I started going into the city, just like the Holy Family . . . No, it ain't easy when a person gets past her prime . . . ain't easy one bit.

Of course, it's never easy for a person to earn a living. And it ain't just us. Everyone has to work for a living. Doctors, insurance salesmen, even people in the government. They all work just as hard as we do, some of them. They're always out on the road, like us, day and night, having to kiss up to people, make promises they know they can't keep, and sometimes . . . sometimes they have to stoop real low. It's not always good, clean work they're up to, them as well as us. I've heard of doctors out delivering two pairs of twins a night, I've heard of farm engineers with college degrees having to stick their noses into a manure pile to see if it's ripe, I've heard of lawyers and government workers — you wouldn't believe what some of them have to do to make a living . . . No, we're not the only ones have to work hard, which is why I ain't complaining. After all, there's some have it worse. It's like I always say, whenever you feel like complaining, La Sagouine, take a look at your fellow man. You'll soon see that life is hard for everyone, and there's always somebody worse off than yourself.

Kind of makes you feel better, sometimes, knowing you got company in your misery.

On Christmas

I may be a raggedy old monkey, but I know a Christian Christmas when I see one. Seen seventy-two of them in my short lifetime, so you'd think that'd be enough to give me some idea, eh? They all look the same anyways, Christmases. Can't tell one from the other. Bells, stars, toys, wrapping paper, angels, Santa Clauses, the crèche next to the shrine, with a nice little manger into it made of thick, grey cardboard that looks so much like real stone you can't hardly tell the difference. It's like I can see it now. Animals stuck here and there to fill in the gaps: ewes, camels, shepherds, a good half-dozen wise men holding their Christmas presents of coal, frankenstein and whatever . . . never could figure out why they thought them things was good presents for a newborn baby, but apparently that's what's writ down, and we don't want to start arguing with the Scriptures, now, do we? Not in times like these.

But Christmas at our house didn't start at the church, it started down at the Irving store. I tell you, in those days I didn't need no calendar from St. Joseph's Oratory to know when Christmas was coming; all I had to do was keep an eye on the window down at the Irving. One day it'd be all lit up, and everything inside of it. Of course it was all fake, like, the cakes and the donuts, even the Christmas tree wasn't real. Not that there weren't enough spruce trees in the bush to go around, but a plastic Christmas tree like that, they said it was prettier than the real thing, and a lot more expensive. Them Irvings, they didn't spare no expense at Christmas time. They stocked up on knickknacks and goodies that'd make your mouth water just to look at them.

We couldn't afford to buy none of it, of course. But it didn't cost nothing to look. We used to watch Dominique's wife when she went in to buy her decorations, her balls and candles and tinsel to hang on her tree. And the banker's kids would buy nuts by the pound, and bananas, too. And big Carmélice, the wife of P'tit Georges, she'd come in every year for her five-pound box of Moirs Triple-X. Others'd buy stuffed bears, and dolls that cried real tears, and electric train sets. There were some kids got whatever they wanted for Christmas and ate oranges till they was coming out their ears.

But the closer it got to Christmas the more people came in from the back country. Oh, they were a wild bunch, they were, you can take my word for that and I ain't lied to you yet. You'd think they'd never seen nothing their whole lives, and now they had to see everything all at once, and they had to touch everything, too. I tell you, they was worse than the people from Cocagne, up in Kent County. Shove over a bit, we'd say to them, give a body some elbow room, but no, they'd stand there taking up the whole space, damn their hides. They'd've taken up Christmas, too, if we'd've let them.

So we'd say the heck with the Irving's window and go on up to the Bingo. Not to play, of course, we didn't have enough money to buy bingo cards for all the games. Just to watch the others play. Every Saturday night and sometimes Sunday afternoons the Ladies of Sainte-Anne, they'd organize a parish bingo to raise money for the poor. So we poor would go down to watch them play. Not for long, mind you, because they had the Sacred Heart League there to keep order, and we'd always end up getting throwed out. Mostly because of the Saint, who never did learn to keep her trap shut. Used to call out to the barber's wife to tell her when she missed a number. Well, there was always something.

And of course we hardly ever missed the pageant. Every year the nuns put on a Christmas pageant with the girls from the convent. They didn't charge nothing to get in and there was a door prize. Different prize every year. One year Polyte's boy got a statue of Petite Thérèse, another time Francis Motte got one of Mary-Queen-of-Hearts, and once the Crotch won a Marie Goretti that was so big she had to leave it in the convent chapel. Not everyone won a statue, of course, but we could always watch the pageant. You knew when you were supposed to cry or sniff because you saw the same pageant year after year. It was good, though, I've got to admit. Towards the end the little angel with pink wings and a star stuck to her forehead would lift up her skinny arms and shout out, "He's come among us to save the poor!" And that's when we saved ourselves by getting out of there fast, because that was the cue for the nuns to start opening the windows to let in some air.

And then on Christmas Eve there'd be the handing out of the presents in the church basement. All the poor got a present, the kids anyways. When you started getting bigger you stopped getting presents, but you could always go to watch. I guess it was the Crusaders for Christ who made up all the parcels, along with the kids from the choir. Go around door to door all through Advent, collecting old toys and whatnots that didn't work no more, and they'd fix them up as best they could. Couldn't expect the mucky-mucks to hand over stuff that was still good, could you? So anyways, on distribution day there'd be a little sermon by the priest that always ended with "Ye must love one another," and that would get the hullabaloo started. There'd be some kid would get a airplane that didn't fly no more, see, and some other kid would get a doll that was supposed to piss her pants but didn't, and they'd start bawling their heads off, and pretty soon the whole lot of them'd be up in arms. Because of course they'd been looking at airplanes that flew and dolls that pissed themselves in the Irving store window for a month, and so they knew what was what. They didn't get presents at home, maybe, but they knew what the darn things was supposed to do. So then the choir kids and the Crusaders for Christ would be all down in the mouth because they'd worked so hard to do a good deed, and the priest, he'd tell them they didn't need to feel too bad because it was the thought that counted. So the upshot of it was, the choir kids would keep coming back year after year to do their good deeds and the poor would keep on getting their busted airplanes.

So anyways, the next day was Christmas. Now, the real Christmas, and I don't mean the Christmas that came from the Irving store, but the Christian one, it got started between sundown and sun-up on the night before Christmas Day. The liquor store would close and after that everyone had to go home. All the houses would light up and pretty soon the whole village looked like a big Christmas tree. Normally about that time we'd be giving the kids a good licking to get them to go to bed, but not that night. That night we'd have to give them a licking to keep them up. Yes, we would. It was the only night of the year the little buggers couldn't wait to get to bed, because of Santa Claus, who wouldn't come down the chimley until they was fast asleep. Now it must've been someone else's kids who put that idea into their heads, but anyways they believed it. Didn't matter how much breath we wasted telling them that Santa Claus couldn't possibly know where it was we lived, and that anyways we didn't even have a chimley . . . they didn't want to hear nothing about that, they'd just drop off to sleep in our arms while we was talking to them.

But they'd wake up soon enough once Noume cranked up his old grammerphone. We'd all get together over at Don the Moose's place, and that's when Noume'd bring out his grammerphone that he brought back with him from Overseas, and which there's some who try to say that no one gave it to him, either, the grammerphone, but then they'd have the Moose to deal with, who'd tell them he'd give them something to remember him by if they didn't shut their traps. So then we'd all get out our records and crank up the grammerphone, and oh, there'd be Willy Lamotte and La Bolduc and "It's a long way to Tipperary."

At eleven o'clock any of us who could still stand upright went to church for Midnight Mass. We'd go a bit early so as to get a good place. Not a place to sit, of course, there weren't enough pews to go around, but they'd let us stand in the back at the end of the centre aisle, because it was Christmas. We couldn't hear the priest say mass because there wasn't room for us in the pews, but we could see the parade when it come in through the back of the church. The priest all done up in his best rig: cassocks and soutanes and so many surplices piled on him you wouldn't think he'd know what to do with them all. And all done up in convent lace. And behind him the younger priests, and then the Children of Mary, then the choirboys carrying the Wax-Baby-Jesus on a pole, all done up in a beautiful lace gown and his hair all curled. They'd take him over to the stable and set him down by the mare and the bull.

You didn't need to worry about the Wax-Baby-Jesus' white gown, because the stable didn't smell like a real stable. It didn't have manure in it or nothing like that, I would have noticed something like that. No, it had a nice crib, made of good clean cardboard with a nice blue silk blanket onto it, and nice clean straw made from excelcis, and the animals were all stuffed and shaved, like. There wasn't no smell of sheep or the barn or nothing like that, except maybe coming from us. We didn't smell all that good, I can tell you, which is another reason we kept in the back. We didn't have lacy clothes or our hair all done up. We could've stood in the crèche ourselves, alongside of the shepherds — that would've been something to see!

Normally we'd leave the church just before the sermon. Not that the priest gave a bad sermon or nothing. He had a voice on him could be heard all the way down the end of the bay, if he wanted it to. But he never raised his voice for Midnight Mass, practically whispered his sermon to the people sitting in the front pews, he was that moved. The rest of us couldn't hear a damn thing he said. And anyways we didn't want to wait and leave with them others because we didn't want to be noticed, like. So usually somewhere between "O Holy Night" and "While Shepherds Washed Their Flocks by Night" we'd sneak on out the front door and go home and finish off Christmas in our own place.

The barn scrapings was real there, I can tell you, and the straw, too. And maybe if we had ourselves a shining star to hang on our door the three wise men might've made a mistake and brought their coal and frankenstein to us instead. But they never showed up. No one did. Christmas for us was like the Bingo or the Irving store: we didn't play and we didn't pay, we just watched other people playing and paying, just like we watched the Wax-Baby-Jesus getting carried straight to his manger, and us, we got to go straight home, same as always.

What if maybe one Christmas the parade took a wrong turn and ended up here at our place, all the shepherds and the wise men and the camels and Joseph and Mary and the little Wax-Baby-Jesus, the whole Holy Family with all the angels and archangels and the mare and the bull, what if they all got lost one Christmas and came here by mistake . . . Wouldn't that be something to see?

Maybe Elisabeth-à-Zacharias, would appear before us from the hills of Sainte-Marie to tell us that one of her nieces was about to have a baby. And we'd run around cleaning the place up, getting the old cradle down from the Saint's attic, making a blanket out of an old comforter. We'd get everything all prepared, ready to receive the baby. Then we'd wait. We'd wait for the angels to come down and sing "Gloria in excelsior day-glo" out on the bay to tell everyone that unto us a child is born in one of the shacks down on the south shore.

And then all the fishermen would come out of their caplin shacks, and the poor would emerge from their hovels, along with the Saint and the Moose and the Jug and me and Gapi, and we'd send for Sarah Bidoche the midwife to be here in case something went wrong. But nothing would go wrong, because everything would take place as it says in the Scriptures, like in a miracle. And we'd go back in to see the Baby Jesus in his mother's arms and Joseph strutting about like he was the father, which they let out he was, or sitting on the flour barrel, with the mare and the bull breathing on the crib to keep it warm. And the wise men would be kneeling in front of him with their presents, only this time they'd be real presents, not coal or myrtle or whatever but something a kid could use, children's toys like a teddy bear or a top that plays Christmas carols when it spins.

We'd be right at home in our shacks and wouldn't be at all embarrassed to take our places among the shepherds and the camels. I'm pretty sure Don the Moose would find something to talk to Joseph and the wise men about. Maybe Gapi would sit down with the menfolk and pass his tobacco pouch over to Zacharias. Yes, I can see that happening. I always thought Zacharias and Gapi had a lot in common; he didn't put his trust in just anyone, did he, and you couldn't make him change his mind about a thing. Yes, sir, he and Gapi would look good sitting on the same bench.

And I can see the Jug going over to have a few quiet words with the Holy Virgin, telling her things, you know, things she wasn't ever able to tell the priest. Or maybe she wouldn't say nothing, maybe they'd just sit there, and they'd laugh together, the two of them, as they looked down at the baby.

And then we'd send for Noume with his grammerphone and

records. And Gerard-à-Jos would bring his juice harp. And we'd all sing a few dirges or maybe "It's a Long Way to Tipperary."

Of course, the Saint would have to join in and sprinkle her vinegar over the whole thing. She might even take it into her head to take a picture of the Holy Family, tell the wise men to stand on either side of the cradle, get all the shepherds down on one knee. One thing's for sure, she'd never see Christmas the same as the rest of us, not her, not the Saint.

Well, and maybe she's got a point, too. If the procession ever took a wrong turn and ended up down in our part of town, it wouldn't really be Christmas at all, would it, because we couldn't properly tart up the front of our shacks with crêpe paper and coloured lights. And we don't have all them bells and stars and gewgaws and plastic Santa Clauses or papier-mâché crèches made to look like rocks so you can't tell the difference. No, we wouldn't know how to receive the Baby Jesus into our homes, would we, not without all that lace and silk blankets and fine crinkly paper for making fake straw. Nope, we don't have nothing to make a nice Nativity Scene out of.

A fine Christmas like that, it wasn't meant for the likes of us.

On New Year's

Yeah, well, it's been a pretty good year . . . Can't complain, anyways . . . a real good year, you can take it from La Sagouine. Ain't been one like it since the year of the big rain, when that Toronto come along and tore all the roofs off the houses . . . Yep, a real good year. No big dumps of snow, no sudden deaths, no one crippled, no one got pneumonia, no water in nobody's basement . . . well, maybe a bit, couple of feet, maybe . . . didn't bother me, though, because I ain't got a basement. No novena of below-zero nights huddled behind the wood stove. Okay, no blueberries, neither, that's true . . . but lots of hawthorn berries and enough beechnuts to choke a horse. Clams were nice and fat and full of mud. And then there was a few weddings, and the picnic up to Sainte-Marie, and the elections. A real good year, all things considered, yes sir!

A good year for the poor, anyways. Anytime you get a mild winter, a good summer for clams, and elections in the fall, well, you couldn't ask for much better than that, could you? You see, take a good cold winter, for example. A person's got to keep warm. Now, if you got cold weather, then you got ice, and if you got ice on the bay, you can cross over it with the sleigh to the cove over there and gather your firewood to burn in your wood stove. But this year, being so mild, like, there wasn't no ice in the bay, and so we couldn't get across it to get our wood out. But we didn't need to anyhow, you see, because we didn't need to crank up the wood stove and sit on it. Worked out pretty good, makes me think there's a special God up there looks after us poor people . . . Gapi, of course, he says it would've been better to have a little heat in the house and a bit of ice on the bay. But that's Gapi, always asking for something he can't have. Like I says to him, you got to be grateful for what the Good Lord gives you. A person can't expect to have everything.

Still, there's them that ain't content with nothing. If the bay don't freeze over then they say the fishermen can't haul their shanties out onto the ice and the caplin'll all stay in the water. Well, caplin are fish, ain't they? Ain't they meant to stay in the water? Yeah, well, we're meant to eat, too, if we're to stay alive. Which is why fishermen wage a year-long war against fish — oysters, caplin, soft-shells, hard-shells, any kind of fish, really, except maybe whales. Haven't heard of anyone tried to catch a whale yet, far as I know. Ha! imagine catching a whale in one of them dories we got around here! Be like trying to pull a camel into my wheelborrow.

I ain't complaining, of course. There's never been a shortage of clams, even when the caplin don't come in. It's like I says to Gapi, it's always a good year for something. You'd think the fish get their signals crossed down there and take turns coming up the bay, like. Which is all right, as long as there's always something to catch, and there usually is. Oysters in winter, and clams, they're like bears, only come out in the spring. Which is why when there ain't no ice on the bay we eat pancakes and beans.

That's something else I says to Gapi. What are you complaining about? No caplin, okay, then you got your stamps, is what I says to him. The fewer the caplin, the more stamps you get. This year we ate on our stamps all winter. I can't see the government letting us poor people go hungry, they can't just stand by and watch us starve to death. No sir. We're entitled, as bondified citizens, according to what the social worker told us. We have the right to eat pancakes and beans the whole year round, if we want to. Of course we don't. No. In the spring right up almost into July we pick mouse-tits, and then there's goose-tongue. We take the small dory out and pick them out on the dunes.

I remember when we first got married we had our wedding party down on the dunes. I'd been picking goose-tongue the whole day, and I kind of threw my back out. Gapi, he always favoured mouse-tits. Been a lot of water passed under the bridge since then, and we still like it, by the jeez we do.

Even though we're entitled as bondified citizens, we don't want for much, I've got to give them that. I get up early and I make a batch of pancakes so we can eat them throughout the day. Come suppertime they've already been warmed up twice, so we eat them with molasses onto them, to bring out the flavour. Then on Saturday and Sunday it's beans. And we all got blankets, too. At night after about seven o'clock I start shoving them into the oven to warm them up. Takes most of the evening, because by the time one is warmed up the first two have cooled down, so I got to start all over again. By the time the kids are ready for bed they're shaking like I was rocking them in their cradles. Once they're all asleep I put them in the same bed, big or small, don't matter, and then me and Gapi we get into our bed. It's got a real mattress with springs into it, too, the priest himself gave it to us, except you've got to be careful where you lay on it or you get them springs poking up into your back.

In August we had a picnic up to Sainte-Marie. Some of us went by boat and some of us by truck. It was François-à-Pierre-à-Jude's truck. Yep . . . a nice yellow one, uses it to haul feed. We had to sit on a pile of clams on the way out and a pile of feed sacks on the way back. But I have to admit it was a nice picnic. They had everything you could think of there: balloons, sparklers, different kinds of poutines, any kind of game you'd ever want to play, squeeze boxes, square dances, bingos, donuts, stew, you name it, it was there. As far as picnics go, this was what you'd have to call a good one. It even had a fall fair going on with the farmers' market. We'd never seen nothing like it before or since.

They had a cattle show, a pig show, a sheep show, oh yeah, you should've been there. Hard to believe, but there's farmers spent their whole year getting their animals ready for the fair. Come down from Sainte-Marie, the poor beasts looking all spooked and nervous like, what with the wheels of fortune and the merry-go-rounds spinning around their heads. Made it hard for the judges to get them to walk in a straight line, two by two, like we used to have to do when we went to school. Still, them bulls and colts looked a lot better off than we did. All well fed and fattened up and pampered to look good for the show. Oh, they was good-looking animals, let me tell you, looked like they never wanted for nothing in their lives. There was one sow there that must've been raised on cream and chocolate, she was that fat. And of course it was her who took home the biggest prize.

Then they gave a prize to the barber for being the fastest in the sheep shearing contest, and one to the rooster who crowed the loudest, and one to the turkey that had the best tail, and one to the woman who made the nicest quilt and to another woman who baked the best molasses cake, and another to the cow that had the biggest udder, and for the ox, and oh yeah, they had a medal for the prize bull, that's what they call the champion stud that sired the best heifers. They brought that one in from way the other side of Acadieville, and they charged fifty cents a head to go into his stall to see him. I didn't go in, not me. But Majorique, old Nézime's son, he got to see it for nothing. He told the fella that was taking the money, he says he couldn't afford to pay six bucks to see a bull, for crying out loud.

"It's fifty cents," the fella says.

"No it ain't, it's six bucks," says Majorique. "I got my eleven boys with me, see, and I'd have to take them in, too."

So when the fella hears that Majorique has eleven kids he says to Majorique, "Stay there," and he goes in and brings the bull out to see him.

That's what Boy-à-Polyte told us, anyways. But you never know with Boy, it might be a true story or it might not.

Then right in the middle of the picnic the chairman jumps up on one of the tables, he must have been a Léger from Saint-Antoine, and he tells everyone to shut up, and then when we're all quiet he don't say nothing. So we're all expecting something to happen, and nothing does, so we go back to shuffling our feet and talking amongst ourselves. And then we hear him blowing into his microphone, and, "Testing, testing, one, two, three . . ." And then of course he starts shouting into it, and he's shouting so loud we can't make out a word of what he's saying. Which don't matter all that much because there's always one of his committee members close by to tell us what it is the chairman is trying to say. Turns out all it was was dinner was being served, chicken stew and poutine râpée.

Yes, a real down-home dinner, you should've seen it, with chicken breasts, whole pots full of them. Everyone in the parish had brought something, because the Sunday before the priest had climbed into his pulpit and told all the ladies to volunteer to come down into the church basement to boil up their poutine râpée and cook up their stews. They all tried to see who could bring the fattest chicken with the whitest meat and who could get the most gravy into their stew. All the parish women standing over their stew pots, it was quite a sight. Each one of them stirring away like mad, adding their gravy and their spuds. In the end they had so much food they had to throw some of it out. Well, they couldn't feed it to the pigs because the pigs were all at the fair. But anyways it turned out there was plenty of good poutines and lots of good stew, and they charged two dollars a head for it. But we took our food that we brought with us so we wouldn't miss out on nothing, and we went behind the school, close enough to the rest but not too close, and sat down on the grass with it. We even brought some beer. And some of us took a little ride on the fairy's wheel. No, we didn't lack for much that day. We went through our pogey cheques pretty fast, I can tell you. The social worker, she said that was no way to manage our affairs, but Gapi told her it was none of her affair in the first place, and that shut her up. She left and we didn't see her face for the rest of the day. Which was all right, our cheques kept coming anyway. Because it was an election year, you see.

In election years they say you never have to worry about getting your pogey cheques or your stamps. That's because the government has more money than usual them years. Don't ask me where they get it from. Gapi, he says . . . but never mind what Gapi says, especially about election times. There's them as says the government is rolling in dough. That sound right to you? They say all you have to do is stick your nose into their books. Well, what do you think? Can you see La Sagouine with her nose stuck into a government book? Yeah, right! . . .

The best thing about elections is that they don't come all that often. Only once every four years or so. Sometimes after two years, but that's only when things ain't going so well, so they ain't quite so generous with the handouts. When one side is sure of winning and the other side is sure of losing, they don't have to make too many promises, neither the one side nor the other. And we're the ones who lose in the end. But when things are a little more up in the air, like they were this time around, and no one knows for sure what's going to happen, ah well! Watch them trot out their promises then. That's one thing that's good to know, Gapi says, it's good to be up on your politics if you don't want to lose out. That's why we keep our noses to the ground, you bet-ter believe it. When they start handing out the grammerphones and the steam irons and the cases of beer and all the rest of it, we want to be right there. They give it all away for nothing, because we're bondified citizens and we have the right to vote. They even come in a truck to pick us up. Yes sir, there's truckfuls of us . . . they don't spare no expense. We get driven around all day in them trucks, drinking beer. And we always end up voting for the losers, because they're the ones who make the biggest promises and give out the best bribes . . . It don't matter much who wins, one side or the other, because once the elections are over they pretty much forget about us anyways. Sometimes they come back asking for their steam irons back, or their grammerphones. Sure, take it all back, we tell them. Especially the beer! Ha! No one who ever ran in the elections has asked us to give back the beer yet.

Yep, it's been a good year. No one dropped dead sudden-like, anyways. Old Jos Caissie's lungs finally gave out, but he'd had the pneumonia for years. And La Célina, she had terminal cancer and never got over it. Ludger-à-Nézime, now, he drownded, but it wasn't what you'd call a sudden death. When he saw his wife wasn't coming back, that she took off, lock, stock and barrel, with her brother-in-law, he got as stinking drunk as it's possible for a man to get and threw himself off the end of the pier. He told P'tit Jean the night before he was going to do it, but P'tit Jean didn't believe him. Told him the water was too cold, he should wait a bit. But that's why he got drunk, see, so he wouldn't feel the cold. That was in April, imagine that! There's still ice under the bridge in April. He might've hit his head on a ice pan, but no, he was lucky that way. Fell between two pans and drownded. His body washed up on shore, all bloated up like a pumpkin. He was that upset, was poor Ludger-à-Nézime, being left on his own like that. Bound to end up bad, in a hole outside the cemetery . . . Yep, that's where they put him. The priest didn't want to bury him in holy ground, said he drownded himself and apparently that's forbidden. Gapi, he says to the priest, forbidden or not . . . once a man's dead . . . But no one ever listens to Gapi.

When a man's dead, it don't matter to him if he's laid out at the front of the church with six candles and buried in holy ground like any other respectable body. That's what I says to Gapi, and I would've said it to the priest, too, if I'd've had a bit more education. Because according to the priest Ludger hadn't paid his tithe, neither, and there was some question whether he'd done his Easter observances. And then to go and throw himself off the end of the pier, and on a Sunday to boot, right under where people was walking, well . . . poor Ludger-à-Nézime is all I can say. A person must be some upset and discombobulated to do what he did. Maybe if he'd known that on top of everything else they weren't going to sprinkle no holy water on him or let him spend his eternity in holy ground, maybe he'd've stuck it out a bit longer and ended up dying a decent death in his own bed. And maybe then the Good Lord would've taken pity on him. Maybe. Who knows? No one's ever come back to tell us. And even when someone does come back, they probably ain't going to appear to La Sagouine. It's not like I'm some kind of Bernadette of Lourdes or something.

No, we're just the wretched of the earth, the lowest of the low. Still, we got no reason to complain. As long as we got our caplin and our crêpes and our beans, and enough firewood from up the cove to keep us warm when it gets below zero, and we don't have pneumonia and we're not dropping like flies, and we've had our picnic at Sainte-Marie, and our election promises . . . well, that's what I'd call a good year, and I hope you had one just like it, damn right I do!

On Lotteries

Jos-à-Polyte just won the lottery! Yes he did, just as sure as I'm standing here, Jos-à-Polyte took home the jackpot. It don't happen too often in these parts; around here you got to grab a piece of luck as it flies by. This is the first jackpot in our neck of the woods since Frank-à-Thiophie won it.

That was a few years ago now, that lottery won by Frank-à-Thiophie, but no one I know has ever forgotten it. Everyone hereabouts has that day fixed in his memory like his own birthday, that's for sure. One hundred thousand bucks, if you can believe it! We ain't used to having buckets of money fall on our heads like that. So when it did happen, a hundred thousand in one go, well it nearly knocked old Frank-à-Thiophie arse over teakettle, I can tell you that. They had to stick his head in a pail of vinegar. I remember because I got the vinegar afterwards and made my pickles with it.

Poor old Frank. He's what you might call the luckiest man ever born in a caplin shack. He never suspected how hard good luck was going to hit him. Not only that, he never even bought the ticket himself. No, it was Dominique's wife gave it to him for spending an afternoon weeding her peas for her. If she'd've known it was the winning ticket she'd've taken off her gloves and weeded her whole garden herself. But how could she have known, eh? Anyways, she said it was hardly fair, a hundred thousand bucks for weeding three rows of peas. Of course, the law had to step in. But for once the poor was in the right.

The poor. It's just a manner of speaking, because after that you could hardly call Frank-à-Thiophie poor. Maybe that's why the law found in his favour. You should've been there, it was all Mister Colette this and Mister Colette that, no more Frank-à-Thiophie, not a hint of it. Now it was Mister François-à-Théophile Colette. And he had to pay the judge and the lawyers, did Mister Colette, and then he had to pay his taxes to the government, right there on the spot, in front of everybody. Course, with a hundred thousand bucks he could afford it, no problem. He didn't hardly miss it.

He could afford a lot of things after that, yes sir, a lot of things. At first, of course, he was so bowled over he didn't know which end was up. But he found out quick enough. Pretty soon there was a whole line-up of people trying to sell him all sorts of things. The first thing he bought, I know because I was there when he bought it, was a tractor. Seeing as how he'd won the lottery by weeding peas, the salesman said it only made sense that a farmer like him should own his own tractor. And what good's a tractor if you don't have a combine? So the salesman sold him a combine, too, one of them big machines that does everything: ploughs, sows, weeds, cuts, picks . . . oh yeah, you gotta say he was pretty well outfitted, was Frank-à-Thiophie, for a man who didn't even own a hayfield.

So of course he had to go out and buy some land, and build buildings on it to keep all his new machinery in. Cost a lot of money, but it wasn't money Frank was short on. Bought himself a washing machine and a refrigerator and a grammerphone, everything electric. We went down there to see him start up all his machines that first night and to listen to the grammerphone. But of course nothing worked. He didn't have no electricity in his house.

It wasn't long after that when an insurance agent came to see him. Now, we'd all heard of insurance agents before, but we'd never actually seen one. They didn't tend to come around here. But after that, well, they sure made up for all the times they didn't come before. Every night a new agent would show up and take a fresh stack of papers out of his briefcase, all written up in advance, and all you had to do was sign your name or make your X onto them and the rest of your life was assured. And every new one was better than the last, so that at the end of six days Frank-à-Thiophie was insured up to his eyeballs and over his head. He had his fingers insured, he had life insurance, flight insurance, fire insurance, he even had his children insured, even though he was a bachelor. It was guaranteed no one could so much as touch him without some insurance company would pay him a lump sum of money. Which of course was all hogwash, because now that Frank was rich no one would dare touch a hair on his head.

Except for the dentist, maybe. The dentist fixed him up with three rows of gold teeth. His mouth was so full of teeth he couldn't hardly chew. So one day he throws his teeth down the outhouse and leaves his face with a big hole in the middle of it, made him look all disfigured-like, poor Frank. And he went to a massage parlour, too, and a choirpractor, and between the two of them they pummelled and twisted more bones than he had in his body, and he came back all crippled up and hunched over.

But it didn't take him long to get over it, old Frank. By spring he'd already started putting on airs. Oh yes! Stopped chewing tobacco and started smoking cigars, and there's even them as was saying — but you can't go around believing everything you hear — saying that Frank-à-Thiophie was rolling cigarettes with dollar bills. Now where's the sense in spreading around stories like that? It's like Gapi says, there ain't no one around here, lucky or unlucky, who'd smoke a cigarette with the Queen of England's

face on it. Anyways, after winning the lottery he didn't roll cigarettes at all, he bought tailor-mades at the store.

Got himself a new set of clothes, too. And he didn't get them
at the Irving, neither. He went all the way into town, he did, said
he wasn't going to go around dressed like everyone else no more.
Clothes make the man, they told him, so he took a look at what
clothes he had and he got rid of them. Sold his old mackinaw,
sold his overalls, sold his old fishing boots that you tie on with a
rope, and off he goes into town. That night when he got off the
bus and walked through the village even the Saint hardly recognized him. He had on a yellow shirt with a necktie, a felt hat,
shoes that clicked on the pavement and a pair of cross-checked
pants, looked like a pansy from the States. By the jumping, if
you put a good set of clothes on a scarecrow you can hardly tell
the difference between him and a senator. Frank got so dandified
he looked like a schoolteacher, so he did. They even give him
glasses to wear, them double-vision kind, you know. He couldn't
see worth a damn but he looked pretty good. People even started
asking him to give speeches. Well, wouldn't you know it but old
Frank-à-Thiophie wasn't such a dummy after all. It's like Gapi
says, nothing like a hundred thousand bucks to smarten a fella
up real quick. I think it was the Richelieu Club that invited
him to their banquet and asked him to say a few words at it.
The Richelieus are supposedly this bunch of rich people that
get themselves all upset over poor people, and they thought now
Frank was rich he'd have something interesting to say about the
poor. And he would have, too, he'd've had quite a bit to say about
the poor, but that was when he still had that jawful of gold teeth
in his mouth and he couldn't say a word, not one word. They
gave him a good round of applause anyways, seeing as how he
was the guest of honour and everything, although he never had
much honour as far as anyone around here could tell.

He'd never in his life had nothing, had Frank. He wasn't used to nothing. But he could learn. A person can learn anything he wants to if he goes at it slow enough. Frank, now, he told himself he could learn to drive. Drive! Why not? Didn't Jos have a garage, and wouldn't he be happy to sell Frank-à-Thiophie anything he wanted to drive around in? And wouldn't he also sell him gas, and oil? Frank had always been a great one for walking. So they started in on him to buy a car. It seems they wanted him to buy Dominique's old Buick, which they said was like new. All they'd had to do to it was put on a new set of tires, change the top, give it a lick of paint and replace the engine; that's why it was like new. Anyways, it didn't stay like new for long, mainly because they forgot to tell Frank where the horn was. So the first night he took it out, after he'd hung his fox tail and his three kewpie dolls from the rear-view mirror and loaded the back seat with all the youngsters on his street, well, maybe he forgot to line up his wheels straight, or maybe his windows was dirty, hard to say, but in any case he swore later that he never saw the nuns' cow. There was a few questions asked, such as what was his like-new Buick doing in the cornfield behind the convent in the first place. But Frank, he just wasn't used to having things, that was what it was. So when he saw the barb-wire fence come up so sudden-like in front of him, it never occurred to him to stop or back up. He was used to only having his legs, see, so he thought he'd just jump over the fence. What they know for sure is, he stepped on the gas. Anyways, the nuns charged him for the cow, the fence and fifty bushels of corn. The garage didn't charge him much for taking back the Buick. They told him that if they wanted to they could have charged him five hundred bucks to fix it, but the Buick wasn't worth that much anymore, and at that price he was better off giving the car back. Gapi, of course, pointed out at the time that . . . Well, you know Gapi, he's always grumbling about something.

It's like the story of the little black kids and the little Chinese kids. This happened when the Missionary Sisters came by collecting for the Save the Children campaign. They had a name — Mr. François Colette, Esquire — and someone sent them up to Frank-à-Thiophie's. Well, they showed him how he could save a lot of souls for the small sum of twenty-five cents, told him he wouldn't have to bother about nothing, not even about bringing the black kids or the Chinese kids over here. They'd look after everything, the Missionary Sisters would: they'd buy the kids, baptize them, raise them up, and save their pagan souls, all for twenty-five cents, imagine that. Of course they also told him that the more pagan souls he saved the more saved his own soul would be. Well, Frank had a few regrets blocking his stomach nights, just like everyone else, so he set out buying up black kids and Chinese kids. Every time he remembered one of the sins of his past life he added a quarter to the pile. After a while it seems he owned quite a few tribes and they were going to make him the prime minister of China and Africa, according to Gapi. And he still didn't feel any less guilty, the poor sinner. Seems no matter how good a person is he can always find another sin down at the bottom of his soul somewheres. Me, I don't think it does us any good to go rooting around down there. Gapi's with me on that. Anyways, as for Frank-à-Thiophie, them African and Chinese babies pretty much broke his bank.

After that he started getting lots of bills. That's because, like, one day he goes to the Saint and says, "If you go get your hair curled I'll pay for it." Well, you know the Saint, she was off like a shot, had every hair on her head up in curlers. She was only sorry she didn't have longer hair so she could have more of it to curl. When Johnny's wife Laurette saw that, well, she got into the act, and pretty soon everybody was getting their hair curled, and Frank picking up the tab. Then there was those who couldn't afford to go to the doctor, or the dentist, or the massage parlour, or the choirpractor, well, they went, and the doctors and such sent their bills to Frank-à-Thiophie. Had so many envelopes going to his place he didn't know where to hide them. And then there was the Boy Scouts selling apples and the priest coming around for his tithe. The priest even mentioned Frank in one of his sermons on the mount, if you can believe it! Thanked him in public for the clock tower he paid for out of his own pocket. Yes sir! Twenty-two beautiful bells it had, all ringing together at the same time and playing hymns from Christmas to New Year's. They call that a carry-on, and it was Frank-à-Thiophie's money that paid for it.

Well, come August month, Frank was leaning on his barrel and he got to thinking. What he thought was, it was high time he bought something for himself, something he'd always wanted, while he still had some of his money left. Up until then, he never had time to think much about himself. But one thing he'd always wanted for himself was a house, a nice big house with brick siding onto it, with an upstairs and a downstairs and a full basement and an attic. And he wanted one with an indoor toilet, and hot and cold running water, and a pantry, and a big dining room, and a summer kitchen as well as a winter kitchen. That's the thing he wanted most, did Frank, a big house with a porch all around of it he could sit out on in his rocking chair and watch the world go by.

So that's what he had built. His own house. He had half a dozen contractors come by with their plans and their carpenters, and they built the whole shebang in two months flat: the attic, the indoor plumbing, the pantry, the dining room and cupboards, three fireplaces, a basement, a summer kitchen and a winter kitchen, and a porch going all the way around the outside of it. It was the most beautifullest house you ever saw, and the biggest, too. People came all the way from Saint-Norbert and Pirogue just to look at it. No one came to spit on Frank-à-Thiophie after that, no sir. He'd made himself a big shot and people respected him for that.

But then one day a couple of months later he gets this big, thick letter from the government in the mail, a big, thick envelope full of pink and green papers with writing all over them, English on one side and English on the other, big writing so you didn't need glasses to read it. And well written, too. So well written no one could figure out what the heck they was on about. In the end, Frank-à-Thiophie, he had to take his big, thick letter to the priest. The priest took him into his office and sat down, and Frank stood across the desk from him and waited while the priest read the letter, and when he'd finished reading it he explained the whole thing to Frank. And when Frank found out how much he had to pay, he realized he was going to lose his house. It was a damned shame. He hadn't been in that house three months.

He didn't have no money left, that was it. Not a penny. And he was still getting everybody's bills coming to him. So he had to cancel his insurance, and he had to sell his machinery, and the tractor, and the grammerphone. In the end they even came and took his telephone and cut off his electricity. He had nothing left. He had to go back to living in his caplin shack. He died there last spring. When we heard about it we all went out expecting to hear the bells tolling for him on the carry-on, maybe a nice Christmas song. But the bells didn't make a sound, because it seems Frank-à-Thiophie hadn't paid his tithe, either.

Well, now, don't you go waiting up for me. I'm going up to pay a little visit to Jos-à-Polyte; I hear he just won the lottery.

On Priests

Now I'm going to tell you something important . . . No, I know it's just a monkey talking, but Sagouine or no Sagouine, I'm going to tell you something. It's not like I done a lot of travelling in my short lifetime, and maybe I ain't seen a lot of things, neither. I'm not saying I know a whole lot. I can sign my name and flip through a newspaper, if it's in French, and that's about it. But I'm going to tell you something anyways, and it's important: It ain't a good idea to speak ill of priests! It's what I'm always telling Gapi, there's no good can come from speaking ill of priests. They're God's presentiments here on earth, priests are, and they can do a lot of harm. You seen what happened to my cousin Caï, eh, and to old Yophie? You never heard two more disrespectable rogues in your life when it came to bad-mouthing priests. Old Satan himself'd have to take a back seat to them two, and if anyone loves chewing out priests it's that one. And look what it's turned him into. No, like I say, priests can do a proper lot of damage.

Now you take my late father, who's been dead these forty years or more and was almost eighty when he died. When he was alive he always warned us when we was little not to meddle in the affairs of priests . . . On account of he knew a few stories that were being spread around the parish about a priest who kept two women living in his house, servants so he called them. Well what of it? my father told us. Can't a man have who he wants to live in his house without everyone making a big to-do about it? Ain't his rectory big enough to hold all the women of the parish and all the men and children to boot? Far as that goes there's room in there for all the cattle and pigs as well. And the whole thing done up in brick, real brick brick, too, not that insult-brick made to look like brick. No sir, if you want to see a real rectory, that's the one to go look at. We can't complain on that score.

In the old days the place'd fill up the first Friday of every month, priests come from all over to hear everyone's confession. Oh yeah, they'd come down from Chocpiche and from Prairie and the Cap and Pirogue and Saint-Hilaire. There'd be so many priests in the village they'd put the whole bunch of us through a fine-toothed comb in no time at all. We'd all be clean as the driven snow by the end of it. It's not a big space, a confessional. About as big as three lobster traps put together. Go ahead, try and fix your mind on the sins of your soul when you're squeezed into a lobster trap. Ha! You can twist around in there all you like, trying to see through the little holes they have worked into them, some kind of wooden lattice thing with a sheet of cellophane behind it so the priest don't catch nothing from you. They say some of them young priests couldn't stand the smell of dirty socks and they'd faint dead away. I guess they weren't used to the odour of our sanctity, poor things. Living up there in that big rectory all year, where the only thing they could smell would be Bon Ami and a bit of lemon oil. Oh no, them priests come from a different class from us.

Anyways, we're not the kind to go sticking our feet under their noses anyways. That's why when the churches got too filled up we just stopped going. We tried to do our Easter observances so we could still be buried in holy ground. And we still gave something for our tithes. I mean, you'd think after doing Easter and giving tithes we'd be allowed into a cemetery at least. As for the rest of it, well, we'd work something out. Or not. Wasn't always easy, I got to admit. Like in confession, for example, when they start going on about firm intentions. Firm intentions this and firm intentions that. Do you have firm intentions to stop offending God? the priest would ask us. Well, it's like he's telling you to change your whole way of living. How does he expect us to do that, eh? Change our way of living, well sure, if we could afford to do it we would. If we didn't have to work so hard that'd be another way of living for a change.

Like I say, it ain't that easy, in fact it ain't easy at all. Like when they says to us, they says, "Stop making homemade beer in your cellars," well, where do they expect us to make it? It's not like we can afford to drink anything else. We can't go out and buy wine or rum, or any of that stuff that comes in a fancy glass with a cherry floating on top of it, what do they call that? No, it's homemade beer from our own cellars for us or it's nothing at all. Then they tells us, "No swearing or performing sinful acts before the children." Well, as for swearing, I says to him right there in the confessional, I says, "You got a point there, Father," I says to him. "How can I swear, by the Jesus Christ, when I can't hardly even speak English?" And as for the other thing, the performing sinful acts before the kids, well, again, where . . . ? When you ain't got but two beds in the house and they're both practically stacked up one on top of the other. I mean, we put out the lights, but . . . it ain't that easy.

It ain't easy to explain to a priest, in any case. We're not highly educated, you know, we don't know a lot of big words, and so we don't always know how to talk to priests about things like that. When he's up there giving his sermon, a priest can sound like the doctor's wife, trotting out all them long words and turning all them fancy phrases. Illiterature, is what they call it. Now us, we never saw a scrap of illiterature in our lives. We use the words that come out of our mouths and that's it, we don't go chasing around after different ones. We got these words from our fathers, and they got them from their forefathers. Passed them on from yap to trap, as you might say. Which is why we find talking to priests so hard.

I wish I could explain to them why it was my daughter didn't get married that time. How could she when she didn't even have a pair of shoes to put her feet into? Anyways, it wasn't her turn for the white dress. There was only the one wedding dress in the whole village, and the Saint's girl had just published her banns. My Angélique had to wait her turn. And by the time the dress was ready she was already showing and she couldn't get into it no more. Had to wait for the baby to be born. Well, it turned out it was twins, and when her fiancé saw that he lit out like someone stepped on his tail. So Angélique, she had to go looking for another one. Well, you try and find a young man these days who'll give up everything he's got so's he can take care of a pair of twins, eh? And twins that ain't even his . . . No, you're darn right it ain't easy. And by the time you get out of the confession box after confessing all your own sins as well as those of your husband and all your kids, well, you ain't exactly looking forward to the first Friday of the next month, I'll tell you that for nothing.

And the poor priest, too. You got to figure it can't be that easy for him, neither, having to figure out what it is you're trying to tell him. He wasn't raised like the rest of us. Oh, they may not all have been born with a silver spoon in their mouth, but they probably always had three square meals a day, most of them, and they probably always had a bed to sleep in at night. And for sure they got an education. So there he is, the priest, thinking we're all going to go in there and behave just like anyone else. He even said as much one Sunday, when he goes up into his pulpit and tells us that before we can get a clean soul we have to have clean bodies first. That's what he says: no cleanliness, no godliness. Well, how does he think we're going to stay clean for twelve months a year, living in a fishing shack all winter and picking clams and oysters out of the mud all summer? No, he's got to get out more, that one, see a bit of life. But what it means is that your soul, well, it's like everything else. You can't count on it. You can't count on nothing, really.

Except maybe on yourself, to look after yourself, to make your own way in life. That's why it's so hard. You don't always know what's best, and there's no one around to tell you. Oh, you know there's laws and certain rules of behaving, and you've got to rely on those, but sometimes . . .

You never knew old Desroches, did you? Used to live up the Amoureux Road there, been dead quite a while now. Well, he spent a good deal of his life outside the church on account of he was excommunioned from it. Yes, and a terrible thing it was, too. I remember how it happened, and then my father, he used to talk about it, too.

It was the thunder's fault, is what my father used to say. You see, the thunder burned down the church. There's them as says it was old Dollard's ghost that rose up out of its coffin and set the fire, and then there's others say it was the priest himself that did it. But you can't go around listening to what every drooling idiot that lets his lips flap in the wind has to say. No, my father, he always maintained it was the thunder that started the fire and should be blamed for burning down the church.

Anyways, however it happened, the church burned down and we had to figure out a way to get it rebuilt real quick. Of course, this time the folks from down the village there said we should move the church closer to the bridge because that's where all the shops were, and the post office. And them from out around the bay wanted to keep it on the Point because they said it was closer for them. So what's your opinion? Is it better to put the church where the most people are, or where you think the most people will come to it? Hard to say, ain't it? Well, there was a big fight over it.

Now people fought about a lot of things in them days, it's

true, and if it had stopped there no one would've minded too much. But of course it didn't stop there. It was old Desroches who'd built it, the church, I mean, the one that burned down. He built that church and he carved it with his jackknife, and he almost felt that the church belonged to him. Well, you go take a man's church away from him that built it with his own hands and carved it with his own jackknife, and you burn it down, and then you move it down to the bridge without so much as giving him any say in the matter . . . Oh, he shook his fist in the priest's face, he did, old Desroches, and the priest had him excommunioned. And for the rest of his life he lived outside the Church.

Now I ain't saying that a person has the right to raise his fist to a priest, I ain't saying that. And I ain't saying the bishop wasn't in his right mind to excommunion a Christian and deprive his soul of everlasting salvation. What I will say, though, and what my father used to say, too, is that old Desroches was not a bad man, and it's a damn shame that he's going to burn in the fires of Hell for all eternity just because he lost his temper one night out on the Point. That's what I mean when I say it ain't always easy to know what's right. And a person might want to ask himself in the end if it's always true that the Good Lord speaks to us through the mouths of priests.

One time there was a priest who came here from the old country on what they call a mission. Seems they came over every year, but we never went to see them, no, I mean if we didn't have nothing to put on to go out amongst ourselves, how were we going to get dolled up enough to show ourselves to a pack of strangers? But this one, they said, wasn't like them other ones, this one was different. He was a saint, they said, a real saint, like you could stick up there on the altar. They said he could perform miracles. Well, we thought, we have to go see this for ourselves. And God is my witness, no sooner did we walk into that church than we knew it was true. That priest recognized each and every one of us! "Blessed," he calls down to us from up in his pulpit, "blessed are the poor and the famished and the badly clothed and them as has spent time in prison." Well, we didn't think we was as blessed as all that, but anyways, we'd seen what we'd come to see.

Oh, he was a holy man, all right, make no mistake, he was the real McCoy. When you get a man who'll walk barefoot in the snow and never take a bite of meat unless you force it on him, and all because he made some vow not to, well then, that's a real saint for you, and you can put him up on the altar just like he is, not even dead yet, by the jumping, yes sir! And talk! Sweet Jehosephat, that man could talk the ear off a brass monkey. He could preach you a sermon for three hours at a stretch and you could've heard a housefly buzzing up the centre aisle. He knew how to tell stories of Noah and Jonas so you'd think it was you who was stuck in the belly of that whale during the Great Flood, yes sirree. And then he'd say something long in Latin, make you think he first come into the world in Nova Scotia or something. Oh, he was a real saint. And all the town women fighting over who was going to have him over for dinner. They all had something they wanted him to touch, they all wanted their own personal miracle from him. The rest of us were just plain out of luck, I guess, because we didn't have nothing to offer him to eat. Once, though, I did get to talk to him through the bars of the confession box. That's when I learned it was even harder understanding him than it was one of our local priests. This mission priest, you see, he only knew about sins from Quebec.

On the other hand, there was one of them came here once, he wasn't exactly a priest, he was what they called a White Father. That's because he wore a white soutane, you see, although I don't know, maybe that meant it wasn't a soutane. Anyways, we never once saw him taking confessions, or giving a sermon, or even collecting tithes. And he wasn't what you might call a saint, neither.

He didn't go around barefoot and he'd eat anything you put in front of him, baloney, sausages, you name it. I know because he came over to our place for supper once. Nothing fancy about that one, no sir. He wasn't a picky eater, and he didn't stick out his little finger when he drank his cup of tea. He ate with us, talked to us just like I'm talking to you, he even played cards with us. And if anyone got a letter from the government or a warning from the police, it was him who looked after it. He didn't go handing out his mother's old clothes, neither, or some broken-down old chairs they had up in the rectory attic. He helped Gapi shingle the roof and stack duckweed around the base of the shack and split firewood for the winter. But he wasn't a saint. He didn't perform no miracles, at least not that I was aware of, and he didn't go around telling us stories about saints, although he knew a few good ones. When it came time for him to visit our house it was like getting a visit from my own father, or maybe from the Moose or Pierre-à-Calixte. We never felt embarrassed in front of him, you know what I mean? He never cared a hoot if the beans were left over from the night before, or if we didn't have the storm windows up, or there was no tablecloth on the table, or we didn't have a brick chimley. He was what you might call a man just like any other man, was Father Leopold. We never had to pretend we didn't have head lice or fleas whenever we saw him hiking up his soutane to step over our fence.

Then one day he just up and left. Went down south some-where to convert the heathen, so he did. It's like Gapi said, maybe if they thought we was heathens they might send us someone like Father Leopold, too, to talk to us and tell us not to worry about last rites, he'd send us straight off to Heaven whenever we dropped dead. Oh well, we can't all be heathens, I guess. Some of us have to wait our turn to see if anyone's going to be holding the pearly gates open for us when we finally get there.

On the Moon

Nope, no one's ever going to make Gapi believe they sent a man to the moon. A man, with two legs, two eyes, ten fingers and one nose, walking around on the moon? What do they take him for? No, he won't swallow it. Frogmen, okay. Baboon-men, well, if you say so. But a man on the moon, save your breath. Don't matter what nobody says, Gapi ain't having none of it. Sure, I told him the newspapers showed a picture of the guy on the front page, up there with the moon under his boots, all in living colour and everything, but no, it don't matter what nobody serves up, including me, Gapi ain't swallowing it. It's all a lot of propagation, he says, they're just saying it for propagation. A man on the moon! When do they think he was born, yesterday? All right, I says to him, never mind, don't go getting your suspenders in a twist. If you don't want them to go up to the moon, well then, they won't go, and that's the end of it. Oh, I tell you, sometimes he's a hard man to talk to, is Gapi.

Man was made to walk on the earth, he says, and sometimes it's hard enough to do that without having to go traipsing around in the stars. And what do they want to walk on the moon for anyways? Eh? Why would anyone want to go there? There's no food there. They said so themselves. The cabbage or turnip that would grow in the ground they have up there hasn't been invented yet. Nothing but sand and rock is what it is, not an acre of good land to be had. So why on earth would anyone want to go to the trouble of landing on something that ain't even land and can't even grow enough food to live off of for one day? If they didn't try to plough up the beach because it was nothing but sand and sold it to the Irvings for a few measly bucks, do you think for one minute they'd go to all that trouble to get to the moon? . . .

I tried to tell him to calm down, no one's arguing with him, there's no need to shout. But he was hopping mad. He just wasn't going to let anyone tell him they shipped a man up to the moon.

The other thing he couldn't believe, Gapi, was that the fishermen from around the bay all sold their portion of the beach. All right, he says, so they couldn't plough it up and put in a field of potatoes, and they couldn't cut wood off of it. Maybe it was just a sand dune, like they say, but it was their sand dune and they had no business selling it. Because they couldn't've sold it unless there was someone willing to buy it, could they? And why would someone want to buy it if it wasn't worth nothing? According to Gapi, if someone wants to buy your shirt off you, it's because there's something in the pocket that's worth something, and you'd be better off keeping it. If the sand in that dune was worth something to the Irvings, he says, it was worth something to us. Of course, he can talk like that because he never owned a square inch of the dune himself. And he sure didn't have any qualms about selling that old plough he got from his father when the old man kicked the bucket, did he? No, he didn't.

It's all a bunch of propagation, according to Gapi. That's all the governments think about, is putting out propagation and trying to get the rest of us to believe it. Well, they won't make Gapi believe none of their stories, that's for sure.

Now, you take the moon, he says. The moon belongs to all of us. Where would we all be if we all suddenly took it into our heads to cut ourselves off a piece of the moon? Eh? If we can cut down every tree in the county to make parks and sawmills, just imagine what we could do to the moon. We'd shave it down so's there wouldn't be enough of it left to bring in the caplin. And why should the moon belong to one of us more than to another? The moon's like the air we breathe, no one's got the right to take it away from us. Gapi says he wouldn't be surprised if one day they tried to sell us moonlight. Just like they already sold us the water in the sea so's we could go fishing.

I got to admit he has a point there. First they sell us fishing permits, and then they tell us we ain't permitted to fish the whole year. The sea belongs to them, I guess, just like the land and the bush. Nothing much left for us, is there? Oh yeah, there's snow. The snow's all ours, go ahead, take as much of it as you want. And wind, too. Wind, snow, cold, water in the basement, help yourself. The sea don't belong to us except the part that comes up into our basements at high tide. That part's all ours, and we can do anything we want with it. Of course, the part of the sea that comes up into the basement ain't the part that has lobsters or salmon in it, is it? No, it's just a lot of foam and mud. If it was worth anything, do you think they'd let us have it for free?

According to Gapi, he says that if anyone went to the moon, from then on the moon would belong to them, just like in the old days land belonged to whoever it was who discovered it first. I told him it don't work like that anyways, never did. Land didn't belong to whoever found it, it belonged to whoever was strong enough to take it from the other fella, or rich enough to buy it off of him. If land belonged to whoever got to it first, how come we still don't have the fifty acres we all got when we first came here? And how come we can't fish year-round in the bay no more? And how come we can't hunt for partridge and porcupine no more in the bush? The land belongs to whoever is strong enough to hang on to it.

Or to whoever hangs on to it long enough. Because sooner

or later, everything comes to him who waits for it. Take Jude's boy, now, if he'd've waited a bit longer, if he hadn't lost his nerve and cut bait, he might still have his bus and be making a decent living today. He'd've probably been able to keep his family living on their land here in the country. But no, he had to go and give up. As soon as he felt he was losing ground a little bit each day, and losing money to boot, he got scared. He could've borrowed the money to get the bus painted and put better seats into it and hire one of them drivers who dresses up like a policeman. And he could've made the long run down to Sussex and Saint John so passengers didn't have to change buses here in town. But all that would've cost money and he would've had to go into debt, and around here you think twice about going into debt, see . . . So anyways, along comes this fella from the States with money to burn, and he buys a brand-new bus with eight tires onto it, and them plush seats with ashtrays in the arm rests and everything, even an outhouse in the back of it. Oh yes, that was one heck of a bus, all right, there's no denying that. And pretty soon everyone's taking that bus instead of Jude's son's bus, because of the out-house and the plush seats. And the next thing we hear is Jude's son's gone and sold his bus and he's working someplace down in the States. And so now we have to take the Yank's bus when we go into town whether we want to or not. If only he could've waited for a bit, you know, held out a little longer, maybe things would've changed for the better, you never know, maybe he could've put an outhouse in the back of his bus or something . . . Well, anyways, it's never easy, is it? Not for someone who's never had nothing in his life before.

Sometimes when things get rough, you know, a man that has a bit of land under him just has to hang on to it and wait out the storm. He has to tell himself that it's just a bit of wind and it'll die down eventually. But no, he's got to have everything right away, he's got to feed his family. So he sells off an acre here, an acre there, and then he sells his woodlot, and then he wakes up one morning and all's he has left is a field full of weeds, and pretty soon he has to sell that to anyone who'll take it off his hands. And you can bet he's not going to get top dollar for it, neither. And then you'll often find that it's one buyer who's been going around buying up everyone's land. Well, where'd he get so much money? Because when a man's got a lot of money, he's got a lot of money and that's it, and you don't think to ask yourself, well, where'd it all come from? A rich man is a man who has a lot of money, period. It's just that when times are hard, like they are now, everyone has to sell his last scrap of good land and then either get his papers for working in the States or else go on unemployment. Then one day you realize that pretty near the whole county belongs to one man. And that man can pretty much do what he wants with it.

He can let it all go back to bush if he wants to, after our ancestors spent the past six generations clearing it. Yes sir, darn near two hundred years of cutting trees and pulling stumps, like my dear dead father used to tell me, and now they're up there planting the land all back into spruce. Pretty soon there won't be a village left in the country, nothing but trees like it was in the old days when there was just Indians living here. The Indians, now, they knew how to live in the bush, they felt right at home in it. They built their lodges in it, they hunted for beaver and partridge. Oh yes, they lived in the bush like they owned it. Not us, though, we don't own any part of it, not any more.

All the land around here is owned by people who bought it up, bit by bit. And once they own it they can stop anyone from fishing in the lakes or in the streams, they can stop us from picking blueberries and blackberries in the swamps, they can tell us we can't have none of our little outings in the bush, they can put up them No Trespassing signs anywhere they want to. And before you know it there ain't a square foot of land or water or even a side road you can stop on to do your business without having to pay someone for the privilege of hiking up your skirt. And that's what it'll be like on the moon, too, according to Gapi.

Anyways, they can have the moon for all I care. Let them figure it out. I doubt any of us are going to want to go up there for a piss any time soon. The rest of it's none of our affair. Which is just as well, as I said to Gapi. As long as they're messing about up there they'll leave us alone down here. Let them squabble over the moon all they like, I says to him, let them squabble wherever it is they want to. All it means is they won't come around here to squabble with us. Let them fight amongst themselves, I says, in Egypt or Vietnam or anywhere they like . . .

Well now, Gapi, he don't even believe they're fighting a real war in Vietnam, that's how stubborn he is. Just a lot of made-up stories, he says. You don't fight a war like that, according to him, and he knows what he's talking about there, because he was in a war in the old country. And what he says is, from what he's heard about Vietnam, it can't happen like that. You fight a war between two armies, he says, on a battlefield, not in the streets and in the schools, where there's women and children. And why would the States go into Vietnam in the first place, is what he wants to know. They don't live there, they ain't so much as stuck their noses in there before, what kind of dumb-ass American would want to go fight on the other side of the world in a war that has nothing to do with him?

"Well if that's so," I says to him, "what were you doing in England?"

"I was in England because I was circumscripted," he says.

Well, I says to him, maybe they circumscripted the Americans, too. But you can't change Gapi's mind by talking like that. There's no way he's going to believe they're fighting a war over there. And even say the Americans did go to fight in a place the size of Vietnam, he says, which is not much bigger than Cormierville, when you get right down to it, wouldn't you think the war would be long over by now? And I guess he has a point. The Americans aren't in the habit of having long, drawn-out wars, are they? That time they dropped their Titanic on Japan, by the holy jumping, there wasn't a cat left alive in the whole country. So how is it they're dragging their feet in a country the size of Cormierville and farther inland than Saint-Norbert and Saint-Paul? You know what Gapi says, he says it's all propagation. So what, I says, let them go at it. When all the soldiers are dead and all the bombs are gone off, then maybe we'll have some peace around here. And as far as I'm concerned, it's better happening over there than over here.

That's what the government must think, anyways, that it's a good thing the war ain't happening here. That way there's no danger to us, you know what I mean? If they have to go dropping their bombs and training soldiers to shoot straight, there won't be no damage done around here. It's the people over there who'll get all the damage done to them, the women and children in Vietnam. Don't know what they ever did to deserve it, though. Don't know at all . . . It's probably not given to common folk like us to know about things like that. I mean, it's not as if the government's going to come down here and explain why they went to war or why they won't let us fish in the sea no more. I don't expect that's any of our business, either. The way I figure it, the people being killed down there must be people like us, and I doubt they were given any say in the matter. They must have brought the war down on those people's heads just like they came here and smashed our lobster traps on the beach, without warning or so much as a by-your-leave. That's government business, and it ain't none of our business, and there's nothing we can do about it. The same as with the people in Vietnam. Anyways, once you're dead there's damn little you can say about it one way or the other. And don't think they don't know that.

But Gapi, he still has something to say. And whether he did or not he'd still be cranky about it. He has no intention of letting himself be circumscripted into another war, or to the moon either, for that matter. If they're that mad to go to the moon, he says, then they'll have to go without him. And he won't budge on that, I know him too well.

So, okay, Gapi ain't going to no moon and that's the end of it. Well, who's asking him to? No one. And I don't expect anyone's going to ask me to take a little spin up there, either. But if they did . . . you know, a short visit, just to have a look around, see what it's like to be that close to Heaven, see a place that hasn't been wrecked yet, that hasn't had all its valuables taken out and sold, that still has its woods and you can pick all the blueberries you want and the beaches are all still thick with clams! Well, I wouldn't mind seeing a place like that! And to see the earth from a distance, hanging up there in the sky, turning and turning, day and night, with all the people in the world on it. From a distance like that a person wouldn't be able to see the mud flowing in the creeks, or the poison ivy in the woods, or see the couch grass, or hear the thunder and the shrieking of the wind. Or the screaming of the kids. On the other hand, you wouldn't be able to hear them laughing, neither, or calling out each other's names. And you wouldn't see the geese returning in the spring, or taste fresh spring water running down the creek beds to the bay.

Yeah, well, maybe Gapi's right. Maybe we're best off just staying where we are.

On Pews

Not that Gapi's a big talker. He's more of an ideas man. But when he does open his mouth to let you in on whatever's going on inside that brain of his, well, you'd better batten down the hatches, because you can bet some priest or revivalist or someone's going to get served up something they're not going to like. That's because Gapi's practically made of bile. He's what they call bilious. Sometimes he comes all over yellow as a turnip, he gets so bilious about things. Well, each to his own, I always say. They say my natural colour is usually green. Séraphine with her crock of homebrew is almost all the time red, and the Saint, she's been pretty much blue since the time she managed to get herself accepted into the Children of Mary, if you can believe it. Can't you just see the Saint as a Child of Mary? Son of a bitch is more like it. Ain't it marvellous how some people get these big ideas into their heads at times? She'd have had herself made a full-blown nun if we'd have let her, I do believe she would.

Like I say, Gapi don't talk much, but when he heard that, he opened his lips and let loose one of them speeches of his there ain't a damned bishop in the country could have spit out better.

"By the Jesus, Joseph and Mary and all the blessed virgins and holy martyrs in Heaven," he says, "what is that woman using for brains!"

Because Gapi might be a bilious, bad-mouthing bugger at times, but he's nobody's fool. And if there's one thing he can't

69

abide it's seeing a man, or in this case a woman, who doesn't know how to keep her place. Now, when Willie's young lad made it all the way into grade eight we didn't say a word, not even Gapi. Go on, we told him, get yourself an education, but don't come around here afterwards writing Latin words on our out-house. "Vincit" is what he wrote, or some such filth.

So imagine the Saint, who to this day has her ribbon and her medal, and as sure as I'm standing here she spends her Saturday nights ironing that ribbon and rubbing that medal with St. Joseph's oil. Ain't how she used to spend her Saturday nights, I can tell you that, which shows you how much this Child of Mary busi-ness has changed her. You'd hardly recognize her now, and you sure wouldn't take her for a woman from these parts. And that's what got Gapi's bile all stirred up. Child of Mary or no Child of Mary, he says, it don't give you the right to carry the big Goretti statue in the processional, and it sure shouldn't make you think you have the right to your own pew in church.

Now I ain't saying we never had no fights before the Saint came along. I'm sure there must've been a few men in the old days who'd beat each other up on the beach or behind the black-smith's shop. But we never saw fighting down the centre aisle of the church before, I can tell you that. And it was the Saint who started it all. Well, what are you going to do with a Saint, eh? And it looks like we're the ones who are stuck with her, too. Anyways, she gets it into her head one day that she's got as much right to go to Heaven as the next person, and she won't be con-tent with being stuck in a closet or a cellar, neither, but she has to take her place like anybody else up there with the saints and the angels and the lambs of God and the whole crew, and she wants that in writing. She wants to be guaranteed a good seat on the Other Side, so she can see everything. And that's why she converted herself from her former ways and got herself into the Children of Mary, which was all right with us, I guess, nothing wrong with that. But then she gets it into her head that she wants her own pew in church. Well, I ask you . . .

There's always been them as had their own pews, of course, and them as had their chairs in the back, and others who all they could get was standing room only. Each to his own, like I said. Nobody got too excited about it. But then the next thing you know it's August and the priest is up in his pulpit announcing that the following Sunday there's going to be an auction sale in the church. Seems he had a bunch of farmers come down from the hills, talking to him about something they called favouritism, saying it wasn't right that the same ones got to sit at the front all the time, and that in their opinion the priest ought to auction those front pews off at an auction sale. Well, let me tell you, that idea went over like a lead balloon. Pretty near the whole parish was against it, all except the farmers and a few others from away. The rest of us didn't have much say in the matter, though, because we hadn't paid our tithes, and around here if you haven't paid your tithe you generally find yourself on the outside looking in.

So anyhow, we was all in church the next Sunday, on account of the auction sale. We never miss an auction if we can help it, because it doesn't cost nothing to go to unless you get stupid in the head and decide to bid on something. And that hasn't happened since Polyte's boy called out, "One dollar!" at an auction sale up to Saint-Norbert, just to cause trouble, like, and didn't Polyte end up with a chamber pot under his arm. Since then we go to auctions, but we keep our traps shut. So there we all were one fine Sunday in August to see them sell off the church pews.

It started peaceful enough, with the processional and everyone wearing nice clothes and going from the main altar to the little altar on the side. And when they got there they opened up the Blessed Sacrament and left it open like that all through the auction sale. The priest, you see, wanted the Good Lord Himself to keep an eye on the auction and make sure no pew went for less than five dollars. As Gapi said later, the Good Lord must've been a sharp businessman in his day, because He sure cleaned up that morning. Oh, you should've been there. I heard that the very front pews, the two on either side of the centre aisle, went for more than thirty bucks, and I can believe it, too, because it was Dominique's wife bidding against the wife of the doctor. Do I hear five bucks, five, now ten bucks, do I hear twelve, twelve bucks, eighteen, eighteen going once, eighteen going twice, eighteen dollars? Sold! So you move up a pew, with a price like that. And then when the barber saw what was going on he wasn't going to stay behind Basile-à-Tom, who'd already moved up a couple of pews. And then big Carmélice plunked herself right in front of Jean-à-François and he decided to cross the aisle and try his hand bidding against the Michauds. But the Michauds had been sitting in their pew since the Expulsion and had no intention of letting it go. Eight dollars, do I hear twelve? Twelve going once . . . Thirteen! Thirteen going once, going twice, going three times . . . Sold! Sold to Jean-à-François-à-Boy-à-Thomas Picoté, that is, not to the Michauds, and that's when it really started to hit the fan.

Lucky for the rest of us we were up in the choir loft, because we knew something was about to happen. No way the Michauds were going to sit still for that, and we were right, the whole lot of them got up and moved over to the Colettes' pew, no warning, no nothing, and by the time the Colettes got wind of what was going on it was too late to stop it: going once, going twice, going three times, bang! Sold! Well, that got the Colettes on their feet, and they took over the Maillets' pew, and the Maillets they took the Légers', and the Légers were all set to kick out the Robichauds when we saw one of the boys from out back of Saint-Hilaire, Frank-à-Louis-à-Henri-à-Bill, I think it was, coming down the middle of the centre aisle. Now there's a family never sat in a pew in their lives before, but what's he do? He yells out so loud he got the stained-glass windows vibrating: "Fourteen bucks!" he hollers.

When the Légers and the Robichauds realized what was going on, they were so flabbergasted they couldn't speak for two-three minutes, and that's when the families from out behind God's back all came down and got pews. Because when the folks from Village-des-Collette saw everyone from Saint-Hilaire invading the pews, they came down, too, and they took over the ones belonging to the Gallants, the Barthes and the Landrys. Then people from the Cove came down and ousted the Bourques, and a group from Petite-Rivière threw out the Cormiers, the Girouards and half the Leblancs in the parish. No one was left but the Richards, and they were sitting hard in their seats with their hands gripping the back of the pew ahead of them, like they'd decided they'd rather have their fingers chopped off than let go. Well, they got the rug ripped out from under them and the wind tore out of their sails, too, and by none other than the Saint herself, if you can believe that.

Yes sir, the Saint, all flesh and bones, body and soul, blood and guts, without a second thought or so much as a by-your-leave, marches right up to the altar almost and right there and then buys herself a pew. And whose pew is it? Well, it's the Richards, ain't it, who's owned that pew since the parish was first founded.

And that's when we figured that everything had gone out the window, and we weren't far wrong. Everyone who'd had their pew stolen from them that morning had a chip on their shoulder, and that was just about everyone. So when they saw the Richards throwing themselves on the Saint, they all joined in, and pretty soon everyone was beating up on whoever was sitting next to them. In less time than I'm taking to tell you about it there was chairs flying through the air, windows being broken, and the

Stations of the Cross coming down on top of Saint Anthony and Mary-Queen-of-Hearts. Even the priest got into it, holding on to his censer as best he could and trying with all his might to protect the Blessed Sacrament. The rest of us were up in the choir loft, clapping our hands and shouting down, "Kick him in the arse, Joe!" Meanwhile, Noume, he got thrown onto the organ and it started playing "Sweet Adeline." I'm telling you, it was the best church service we ever went to. When the priest finally got everyone out of there, they were all hanging on to a piece of their pew.

Except for the Saint. She wasn't hanging on to nothing, not her. Because the very next Sunday, when she put on her hat with the feathers onto it and headed straight for the pew she bought, she found it was already taken. It's all very well to make a bid during an auction sale, but you also got to pay for what you bid on, and you got to pay up, cash on the barrelhead. The Saint, though, she thought buying a pew was like buying a keg of molasses, you could do it on credit. And that's where she went wrong. The Richards had the money right up front, and they got the pew. And it wasn't only her, either, but a lot of them farmers lost their pews the same way and had to go back to sitting at the rear end of the church.

And that's also how Louis-à-Levi ended up with nothing. Poor old Louis! He'd been sitting in the same pew for years and years, up there beside the Sacred Heart right next to the pillar. Ever since his wife died of some kind of lung infection there'd been no one sitting anywhere near him, and he was lonely. All his kids had moved to the States and left him up here all by himself. So whenever he finished his chores he'd come up to the church, old Louis-à-Levi, pretty near every night, making his rounds. Then in the mornings he'd go to mass, and on Fridays and again on Sundays he'd do his Stations of the Cross.

And he had his pew, and a right nice pew it was, too, with

its kneeling bench and a number on the side of it and a little rack where he could put his prayer book when he wasn't using it. It was a real pew, as good as anyone else's in the parish. And it wasn't like he was rich or nothing, was Louis, or that he was all that big-feeling, it's just that having a nice pew made going to church more interesting. And since he spent half his life in it, he thought he might as well have a good one, where he could see what was going on up front but not be bothering anyone behind him, like. Well, anyway, one year he sold a calf to pay for his pew, and the next year the price went up and he had to sell a cow. And before long he'd lost pretty near his whole herd and was reduced to selling off his chickens and pigs. Then came the auction sale. Well, that was the year a farmer from away came to settle in the parish, man by the name of Bourgeois, came up from the south and owned a lot of land, by all accounts. A man like that couldn't just stand at the back of the church during the service, could he? It wouldn't be up to his dignity. So it seems his wife says to him he's got to right off buy them a pew. Well, you can't just up and kick a neighbour out of his pew, a newcomer like that, you have to wait until one comes up for sale. And it wasn't too long after that they had the auction.

Meanwhile, the man's wife had been asking around, trying to find out who wasn't able to pay full price for his pew, and that's how she got her husband to bid against old Louis-à-Levi. Well, the bidding didn't take long, because all Louis had left was a couple of chickens and a goat. And it was the goat he'd had since his wife died, and he didn't want to part with it. So that's how he lost his pew, just like all the others. And now he don't hardly go to church at all no more. There's them as says he spends his evenings sitting beside his split-rail fence, just him and his goat, staring off into space. Makes you kind of sad, in a way . . .

But as for the Saint, that's another story. No one felt sorry for her. She had no business trying to insinuate herself into a world that wasn't her world, trying to live a life that wasn't her life.

"You got to know your own place and stick to it," that's what Gapi says to her. "Them front pews are for people with fur coats and silk neckerchiefs. Them as comes to church wearing gum-boots and mackinaws, they got to make do with the chairs in the back. And the rest of us got to stand, just like we always done."

That's what Gapi says, anyways, and I can tell you there ain't a bishop around who will tell you any different.

On War

It's a good thing we had the war, don't know what we'd've done without it. Talk about tough times! There wasn't nothing happening between the Depression and the war, and I mean nothing. Not a thing. If the war hadn't come along when it did, we could easily have dropped like cows in the forest, curled up in our holes and died. I'd say the war came just in the nick of time. Saved us a lot of grief. Because if we hadn't been able to go off to the war, if we'd just keeled over in our tracks, I doubt anyone would've noticed. In those days, even the rich had a hard time making ends meet, let alone the rest of us . . . The rest of us couldn't even make one end meet. We didn't have two cents to rub together. So it was a good thing the war came along.

Yes sir, it was a darn good war, if I do say so myself. Before that it was as if the Good Lord himself was too hard up to think about us poor folk down here. If anybody'd asked him I doubt he'd have been able to name a single one of us. It was like no one remembered there was people living down here. Maybe that was because for the last few years the only things leaving these parts were children's coffins. Those of us who did manage to stay alive just holed up in our lairs like groundhogs waiting for the spring — and for us, spring was the war.

The war changed everything, especially for us. They sure knew we were here after that. Wasn't three months into it before they knew the name of every man around here, as well as his age, his weight, the colour of his hair, what kind of diseases he'd had and hadn't had yet. They also knew what he did, and how many wives and children he had. It was all written up on their forms, like from then on the government intended to come down here in person and take care of our business for us. We thought it was odd but we didn't complain. It didn't make no difference to us who took care of our business. They couldn't take more from us than we had, and we didn't have nothing.

We didn't even have beds to sleep in. They was the last to go, as I recall. And I'm not talking about box springs and feather mattresses, no sense pretending I am, I'm talking about beds made of planks taken off of all the schooners that went aground on the rocks up and down the coast. They smelled a bit like kelp and seafoam, but they didn't hold water, which was good. We built them high off the ground so they wouldn't carry us out to sea at high tide or with the spring runoff. But in the end we had to let our beds go along with all the rest. You can't eat feathers or a box spring. You can sleep standing up or whatever, but you can't eat wood. Not for long, anyways. Not your whole life. Yes, the war was a good thing.

They came in their jeeps. One morning they just come right up to the houses. We didn't exactly have a six-lane highway going past our place, so they had to come in jeeps. Two nice, shiny jeeps, so powerful they didn't have to bother to stop and open the gates, they just rammed right through the fences like they was clotheslines. All the men came out of their shacks to see what the heck was going on and they came up face to face against circumscription. They circumscripted them right there on the spot, right on their own doorsteps. Then they went around to all the houses to make sure no one was hiding anyplace. Me, I couldn't see why anyone would bother hiding from a war that was taking place in the old country, which was at least a hundred miles away. That's what Gapi says to them, but they went through all our places anyhow, right down to the last outhouse and caplin shack. They didn't find no one, except for old Ferdinand-à-Jude, who'd stayed inside because he had his two legs cut off above the knee during the first war, and 'Tit Coq, who wasn't all there. He got menningjitis when he was a baby, did 'Tit Coq, and like they say you either die from it or go crazy. He wasn't right in the head, the poor thing. Anyways, he was the only one here who was afraid of being circumscripted, so he hid himself in a molasses barrel. Well, they hauled him out of that and circumscripted him along with the others . . . until they found out he had six toes on his left foot, or so I'm told.

They had to let Julien-à-Pierre go, too, and Tilmon, and the Hunchback. One of them had holes in all three lungs, according to his report. The other could only see out of one eye, and whenever they put a rifle in his hands he kept turning around until it was aimed at the sergeant. The Hunchback couldn't keep in step, apparently; it ain't easy going in a straight line when all you can see is the ground at your feet. Poor souls, they was spared, all right, but they came back looking pretty hangdog about it. The army paid pretty good back in them days, and it even sent paycheques to the wives whose men were gone off to the war.

So anyways, we began to crawl up out of our holes a bit. The first cheque that found its way to these parts came to Laurette-à-Johnny, and it was a good thing it came the day her mother looked like she was breathing her last, because the doctor was there and it was him who noticed what the envelope was. Laurette was about to throw it in the stove, thinking it was just some old ad for a catalogue or something. Pretty soon we all started getting them, and none of us threw nothing into the stove after that.

So as far as wars go it wasn't too bad. It was a good war, in fact. You should've been there! Especially when the parade came down the road. We all ran out and hung over the fence for hours watching the tanks and the jeeps and the big guns go by, and calling out names to the soldiers that was playing on the trumpets or beating the drums. Then we tried to march alongside of them. They looked like proper soldiers, all dressed up in their army uniforms or their sailor suits, their heads all shaved smooth. They looked pretty good. Some of them winked at us out of the corners of their eyes because they weren't allowed to turn their heads as they marched. That's why we marched beside them. Of course, there was always some of them bold enough to try to pinch us to make us laugh, until the captain made us get back behind the fence. At least we could listen to the music and watch the parade.

Sometimes on Sundays we'd go watch the Home Guard practising for the war behind the church. Oh yeah. You see, what they did was, they took all the men who were too young or too old or too crippled for the real army, and put them into the Home Guard. The Reserves is what they called it, and they stayed behind to defend us in case the war came here. All the strong ones who were in good shape, they sent them overseas to defend someone else.

They were a good Home Guard, though, I'll give them that. Watching them wasn't like watching the parade that went down the road, it was more like watching a kind of fake war or something going on in the churchyard. There was 'Tit Coq with his six toes, and Julien-à-Pierre with the holes in his lungs, and Tilmon and the Hunchback, and all the old fellas that used to hang out in the blacksmith's shop, smoking around the forge all day. There they all were, joined up and in the Home Guard. They had a sergeant there to show them what to do and how to defend the country in case the Germans suddenly landed down on the beach. That was Telex, who'd been in the other war, the first one, but he couldn't go back to the Front because he'd been gassed the first time, or something like that. Left him kind of bitter, Telex, kind of all shook up like.

But what the girls around here liked best about the war, if you ask me, was the Flat Foots. That's what we used to call the English soldiers who come over here to practise doing the war where it was safer. Well, it stands to reason, it couldn't have been easy for young soldiers to practise their exercises with bombs and cannons going off all around them. It'd be too distracting. Anyways, Gapi had something to say about that. A war should take place at the Front, he said, not behind a church. And what kind of faith could you have in a soldier who had to go somewheres safe to practise? And I suppose Gapi had a point, especially when it came to them Flat Foots . . .

They looked all right, if you know what I mean. They were good looking. There wasn't a girl for miles who didn't want to have her English boyfriend. Even the girls from the better families, didn't bother them at all to be seen with a Flat Foot. But the Flat Foots, they only came here to practise the war, and then they had to go back to where they came from. They left a few broken hearts behind, I can tell you, not to mention a baby here and there. Well anyways, that went on for a few months, maybe a year or two, and as far as I'm concerned a person shouldn't look a gift horse in the mouth even if you only have it for a short time. You take the war, it only went on a few years, but it was good while it lasted. Not too bad at all. It was the best thing to happen around here since the Depression and the shipwreck down the beach.

During the Depression things got so bad around here I don't see how a person could have sunk any lower. When we get that low, at least they always decide to do something to make sure we don't disappear altogether. In the Depression, it was bread lines. After that things started looking up a bit for us. Every month we got our sack of flour and our keg of molasses and sometimes even a bit of buckwheat to make pancakes with. You could say it was the Depression that delivered us from poverty, in a way. The worst time for the poor is when there's nothing happening at all: no war, no floods, no big crash at the market, nothing to remind people that there's some of us who have nothing to put into our mouths. Them's the hardest times, and it's lucky for us they don't go on for too long. Good thing for us there's always some kind of catastrophe happens about once every decade or two, so if we hold out long enough we can usually breathe easier every ten or twenty years.

The last one was the shipwreck down on the beach. There was more than sixty men went out on the cod fishery that morning. Apparently the radio was saying there was a big storm coming, but none of the men had radios on board. Some of them didn't even have engines, had to row themselves out. Anyways, the storm came up behind them, and by the time they saw it they were too far out and didn't have time to make it back to the harbour. They say the waves were more than sixty feet high, and there were men in dories out there. Most of them were driven up onto the beach, masts, dories, men, everything all broke in a million pieces. Fifty-three men lost their lives just like that. Anyways, the priests didn't make no fuss about burying them in holy ground that day. Last rites or no last rites, if you die in a shipwreck that claims fifty-three lives in one go, they're going to bury you in the cemetery reserved for those who die in a disaster. No sir, it's no joke hearing the church bells toll fifty-three times in a single day. But anyways, it kind of put us back on our feet again for a bit, did the shipwreck. There was a write-up about it in the *Gazette* and it was on the CBC, and there were Sunday sermons about it, and pretty soon everyone was taking up collections to help us forget our troubles. Well, at least it helped us forget our hunger. For a while, anyways. Which was still okay.

And after that was the war. I still think it was the best thing that could've happened to us. The very best thing, what with the shipwreck and the Depression, because they just kept on sending us our cheques for as long as the men were overseas. And the women whose husbands didn't come back kept on getting their widows' pensions. And Caillou, who lost one of his legs in England, he got paid more for that lost leg than he ever earned in his life with the other one. And Jos Chevreu, he came back with two holes where his eyes was, and they gave him a pair of sunglasses and a white cane as well as a pension. And then there was the late Pete Motté's son, who hadn't been more than eighteen when he signed up, and who'd been the sole supporter of his mother ever since Pete's death, seems they found him wandering around the battlefields in France two years after the war was over, on account of he'd lost his wits, the poor thing, when a bullet got lodged in his head between the bottom of his skull and his spinal colyum. They brought him home and gave him back to his mother, good soldier that he was, but he still don't recognize her to this day.

Anyways, at least he came back. Can't say the same for the Saint's son: he got married over there and she hasn't seen him since, although she knows he's still alive. They say he won't set foot around here no more, and if you ask me it's because of Jeffrey's daughter. He was dead set on her before he left, and seems she ain't never forgot about him. They were engaged and everything. I doubt he'll ever be able to bring his bride back here, where she could just as easily as not promenade herself up and down in front of Jeffrey's house just to piss off his daughter. No, for sure the Saint's son ain't never going to darken her doorway again.

And maybe it's just as well, when you consider what happened to poor Joseph-à-Maglouère-à-Louis. He was reported dead, and his widow wasted no time in giving up her pension and taking up with the youngest Damien boy, who was a good-looker in his day and had a hot temper. So when old Joseph returns from the war like a ghost and finds the Damien boy in his bed, well, the poor man, they fished him out of the sea that spring along with the oysters.

That was twenty years ago now, and we're up to our necks in misery again. At least the war gave us some work and something to put into our stomachs. We had five or six good years, and then they signed the peace and we had to go back to our oysters and our clams and our quahogs. And times got tough again and the poverty came back. There's only one thing we can do about it, and that's wait for another war to come along and haul us up out of our holes, just like the last one did.

On Funerals

So we buried poor old Joe, set him in his lowly grave. In a manner of speaking; it wasn't as simple as that, of course. In fact it was a lot more complicated than anyone would've thought. A lot more. Well, we buried him, end of story. But oh, poor Joe! You see, we'd made him certain promises. Of course we had! We'd sworn by all that was holy that he was guaranteed a hole in the ground, a nice big hole, big enough for a coffin he could stretch out in, tall bugger that he was, so they wouldn't have to scrunch up his knees or twist back his ankles. A real casket, with a pillow into it and a cross and handles on the outside of it, a nice coffin fit for a man who died with his boots on. That's what he wanted, old Joe, more than anything in the world. And we promised it to him, swore by the Virgin and all the saints that he'd have a coffin so fine he wouldn't be ashamed of being dead in it and laying alongside all the others. Poor old Joe.

It was on account of his remembering his dead father, at least his dead father's first death. Yes, that's right. It's always been said around here that Joe's father, Antoine-à-Calixte, died twice. Just how dead he was after his first death, well, all I can say is he sure enough looked dead. It was when the Spanish flu was going around, and Antoine, he came down with it like a lot of others did. And before anyone even noticed he was sick, there he was, dead and dressed up for the boneyard. They had to move pretty quick in them days so the sickness didn't spread, and that's why no one really took the time to give him a proper funeral, or even sit up with him overnight. They said he looked too far gone and he didn't smell too good, neither. We got to get him under the ground, they all said, he stinks already. Well, that didn't wash with some of us. Old Antoine-à-Calixte stank to high Heaven most of his life, the poor old thing. Anyways, they laid him out in the church, and just when they was singing the Liberace over him the top half of his body sits up in the coffin and shouts out, "Jesus Christ, what the hell is going on here?" At first everyone thought it was the verger who'd come to lock up the church — because of the flu, you see, we'd been holding a lot of funerals after dark — and everyone turned around to look at the back of the church. But then when we turned to the front again there was Antoine's dead body trying to heave itself up out of the coffin and untangle its fingers from the rosary. Seems that when he woke up and realized what was going on, well, he recovered from the flu in a flash, and he never caught another sickness for the rest of his life. It took a clap of thunder to do him in at the ripe old age of ninety-two, a clap of thunder that came down on him like a ton of bricks.

Now, poor old Joe was right young when his father died the first time, and he was never able to get the idea of it out of his head. He used to hide behind the stove on winter nights and listen to his father telling about what he'd had time to see on the Other Side before he came back. Everyone for miles around used to get together at Antoine's to hear him talk about it. He was no preacher, was old Antoine, and he'd pretty much tell people whatever it was they wanted to hear. All you had to do was ask him about someone you knew who was dead, someone in your family maybe, and sure enough old Antoine'd seen him shovelling coal or walking in a procession along with the angels and the lambs. He said he'd seen Pierre Crochu on the Other Side, who was dead, harnessed to the same cart as old Bidoche, and together they was hauling a cartful of devils on their way up here to stir up trouble on All Saints' Day. He also said the devil's cauldron was full of people from around here who we all thought were respectable because they walked around with their noses in the air all the time. He said he couldn't name any of them, of course, because their relatives was still alive and still walking around with their noses in the air. Oh, he was a good talker when he got going, was old Antoine-à-Calixte. He knew how to make you shake in your boots, all right, or bust a gut with laughing so hard. But Joe, he never laughed. Death always gave him the heebie-jeebies.

Seems it wasn't long after that that Joe began thinking about death pretty near all the time. And the more he thought about it, the more he worried that death was going to sneak up on him and jump him from behind when he was least expecting it. He'd remember his father's first death, and he'd want something more respectable for himself, none of this halfway stuff, no partly dead and partly not, no jumping up out of your coffin with flowers on your head and your fingers all tangled up in your rosary. No sir, none of that for Joe. What he wanted was the kind of death rich people have. Rich people ain't buried until everyone's good and sure they've breathed their last breath.

The problem was, Joe wasn't a rich man. As a matter of fact, he didn't have a pot to piss in. And that's what worried him. These days, a good death costs money. You got to get bombed, you got to have a shroud, you got to buy yourself a plot, and a decent coffin, and some decent clothes to go with the coffin. None of that's the kind of thing you trip over in a patch of blueberries, and so far as I know no one ever won a casket or a headstone at the Bingo. Poor Joe, he wanted a good death so bad it was killing him. He was ready to do anything to get it. So that's when he began taking steps. Oh yes, he took steps, all right. And pretty big ones, so they were.

One fine morning he turns up at the undertaker's door, and

he asks him how much it would cost to have himself buried first-class. Nothing but the best for our Joe! First-class or nothing, that's what he said. Well, it came pretty close to being nothing, I can tell you. The undertaker, he looks Joe up and down to see if he was having his leg pulled, and then he rattles off the costs: first the coffin, fully loaded, inside and out, six handles and a silver cross, large- and small-sized candles, wreaths, curtains, ribbon on the door, blowed-up phonograph of the deceased . . . That set Joe back a bit, because he'd never had his picture took in his life. And he couldn't afford to have one took then because he still hadn't bought his suit to be buried in. Anyways, turns out one of his cousins loaned him a black jacket and a white shirt, and poor old Joe, he takes them to sit for his phonograph. They had to go at it three times. Seems Joe didn't want no one going around saying he got his picture took in his overalls, so he puts the white shirt and the jacket on overtop of his long johns and tells the phonographer not to shoot him below the waist. Well, of course each time there was a little bit of long john showing below the jacket. So in the end they had to cut the portrait off just across here, and poor old Joe, he looked like a real dead man in it. I swear to God, it looked like they cut him in two.

Yes sir, a real dead man. But what bothered Joe the most was that he'd already spent more than a thousand bucks and he wasn't even buried yet. He still had to buy his headstone. Oh yeah, if you want a first-class burial you have to have your slab of stone above your grave, a real stone made of real stone, with your name carved into it and your R.I.P. and your date of death. They even asked Joe what kind of death he was expecting to have, because usually they carve that on the headstone, too. Then they put some kind of figurine laying on top of it, like an angel or something, watching over your eternal rest. It's supposed to look good, but it's also supposed to jack up the price. No one, not around here at least, has seen anyone get their eternal rest for free. No sir, a good death, who can afford it?

Then, of course, there's what they call the funeral services. That's the whole burial ceremony, where they have a kind of parade that starts at your house with the neighbours, the family, the priest, the children's choir, the pallbearers and the deceased. Everyone walks two by two behind the coffin holding their noses and sniffling . . . and God forbid that during the funeral services anyone takes a chew or starts to laugh or even looks around to see who else is in the parade. No, you've got to walk along as stiff as the corpse, with your head tilted a bit to one side, and not too fast, neither. You keep your eyes staring straight ahead of you. And you have to wear black to a funeral, you know, if you have anything black, and put a ribbon around your arm, and get out a clean hankie. That's how you follow the parade, not going too fast. Right up to the church and into the churchyard, keeping your eyes down. Then the priest, he buries the deceased in Latin, sprinkling holy water onto him, and you've got to stand still out of respect for the deceased's family. Because the person, as you might say, the dead person, was a living person before he became dead, and he always leaves someone behind to mourn him no matter what kind of son of a bitch he was when he was alive. Rarely does a dead person not leave someone behind, a mother or a brother or a child or a wife, someone who can remember him when he was young and full of beans and went along to funerals like everyone else. And the memory of it wrenches your guts and brings tears to your eyes, so it does.

But it doesn't last that long. No sooner is the Latin over than the gravedigger comes up with his shovel and the priest makes a sign telling everyone to go home. Then we all go back to smoking and whistling and running around and calling out to one another. Once the funeral services are over you can go back to living again.

Still, you can only live out your allotted time on earth. Because one day you know it's going to be your turn, and you can be pretty darn sure you ain't going to be getting one of them first-class funerals. They're going to bury you, all right, but without a lot of pump and ceremony. That's the kind of thought that got into poor old Joe's head, and there wasn't nothing he could do about it. He came back to the village with his fancy phonograph in his hand and he sat down and started to think. He sat there thinking all night. In the morning he went out oystering as usual, and that night he didn't come in with the others. He took to fishing double shifts, did Joe, stayed out there day and night. "Joe," they told him, "you're going to die from yawning." But that didn't make him slack up one bit, it just made him fish all the more. The more he saw death approaching, the harder he fished. Poor old Joe. The other fishermen, they realized that Joe'd fish out the whole bay if they let him, and they got onto him about that. They made him fish further out, at the far end of the cove, and then above the river, where there wasn't too many oysters, and poor Joe had to work twice as hard. Well, that's how they found him one morning, face-down in his dory with his hands twisted around his rake.

That's when the other fishermen started feeling bad about what they'd done to poor old Joe, and what they said to him and all. It was like they'd up and killed him themselves. And then they all remembered what they'd promised him, to not let the worms and the rats start in on him before the funeral was even over. We'd sworn by the holy oil of Saint Joseph on All Saints' Night that we'd bury him in a nice coffin that hadn't been used before, one with handles onto it and a nice lining into it, and all waterproof and everything. There was nothing for it but to stick to our word. But it wasn't going to be easy.

And the reason it wasn't going to be easy was because Joe had a lot of brothers and sisters, and when each of them found out about Joe's death and that he'd been saving up for a big funeral, they started pouring in from all over the place, some from the States and some from Ontario, others from the North Shore all the way up to Caraquet and Tracadie, oh yes, some from as far away as that. We'd never seen anyone with such a big family: brothers, sisters, cousins and second cousins, a whole truckload of them. And they never even went to the church, no sir, they went straight to Joe's place and started ransacking his cabin, his cellar, his boat, and they carried the whole kit and caboodle off with them. Everything! They even took his cousin's black jacket and white shirt. Left him to be buried in nothing but his long johns and overalls, poor old Joe.

That's when Élie had his idea. Joe's relatives hadn't carted off Joe's cabin nor his dory. Those things still belonged to Joe, and they could follow him into his grave. The cabin was made of softwood lumber, but there was no worms in it, which was the important thing. The men went down to it and tore the whole thing apart, board by board, and saved the best planks from it to fix up Joe's boat with. They turned that dory into as good a coffin as you'd see in the attic of any store. Then the women came with their lengths of curtain, and they lined the dory all in red and white polka dots so you could hardly smell the fish at all. Then they made a top for it out of the kitchen table and took the handles off of the stove and put them on the sides. There was only one thing wrong: we was pretty sure the dory leaked like a sieve, because we all knew that poor old Joe spent the better part of his life bailing. The only thing we could think of was to cover it on the outside with brick siding. It was Jonas who agreed to take the siding off of his own house down the south shore. His wife screamed at him all night, but Jonas got it off. And there was poor old Joe with a nice coffin all lined with curtains and covered in brick siding, with stove handles all around and his phonograph of the deceased in a black jacket sitting up on the foot of it. It was something folks from around here had never seen the like of, as far as coffins went.

But that wasn't the end of it. We still had to get him dressed, old Joe. He wouldn't have wanted to be buried in his overalls. You rarely see overalls in a nice brick coffin. So we all gave something. And when everyone had thrown something into the pot, we could finally dress him up. And you can bet that whatever Joe might suffer from on the other side, it wouldn't be cold. You've never seen a man buried with so many clothes on in your life before: three pairs of socks, four pairs of mittens, five shirts, two jackets, four neckties, two pairs of underwear, one sou'wester and three gumboots. All that and the curtains in the bottom of the dory.

So anyways, we led him in a procession down to the church, and we paid to have the bells rung. They rung for a good part of the morning, too, because we paid more than the going rate. Then we dug a hole for him in holy ground, in the shadow of the cross, right next to the nun's section, a hole deep enough that the rats couldn't get to him. As for worms, Elie told me he'd sprinkled the coffin with poison so they wouldn't dare go near it.

In the end we figured he was pretty well taken care of, was poor old Joe. He wouldn't freeze, he wouldn't be eaten, and he wouldn't try to get up out of his coffin, neither, because we waked him for five nights to make sure he was good and dead and wasn't going to come back to life, like his late father. But poor old Joe, he had no intention of coming back. When you have a decent burial like Joe did, you count your blessings and you stay dead. There ain't too many people around here gets a first-class funeral, with a lined coffin you can sleep comfortable in, knowing that no one's going to come and disturb you for the rest of eternity. Damn it, Joe!

On God's Goodness

There's no doubt in my mind that the Good Lord is infinitely good and infinitely kind and that nothing ticks him off like sin . . . And it's equally certain and sure that we are all poor sinners who are extremely sorry for ticking him off. So, knowing that, how do you expect us to die in peace? Is that enough to guarantee a man's eternal eternity? What they say is that when you wear your scapular and you've got your medal and you get your Extreme Unction, you've got nothing more to worry about as far as your guaranteed place in Paradise is concerned. But there's nothing in there says your place is on Saint Joseph's lap or even at the feet of the Baby Jesus of Prague. The way I see it is that maybe you don't get a good seat, but you get in, and that's what counts. Because once you're in Heaven you're supposed to get everything you can ever want, and so whether you get in first-class or tourist, it don't matter.

The same is true for Hell. If that's where you go, what's the difference between a little bit less or a little bit more coal on your bones? If you burn, you burn. You don't burn more or less. That's why once you're on your way there I don't see any use in kicking and screaming. Specially since whatever happens happens for all eternity. And eternity is forever, it don't go on for less time or more time, it just goes on. That's why I don't see any big difference between going down there first-class or last class, being burned forever in a nice big bonfire or in a piddly little bit of flame.

Yes sir, I know that the Good Lord is infinitely good and infinitely kind and also that he's just. He has to be. He wouldn't be the Good Lord without that. I also know I hadn't ought to worry about any of that or even question it, because didn't he already tell us that too much questioning about questions of religion causes you to lose your faith? And once you lose your faith, well, it seems not even Saint Anthony can help you find it again. So you've got to grab onto it with both hands. Take a deep breath, as I says to Gapi, and hang on for dear life. Once you're dead you can breathe easy. You don't have to believe in a thing without seeing it when you're dead, because all things will be revealed to you. But as long as we're alive we got to go with what the cataclysm tells us and believe what the priests teach us and keep our eyes shut and our faith gripped in the palms of our hands like it was the key to Paradise.

We just got to wait to get the answers when we're on the Other Side, is all. But once we're there, we're going to understand a lot. We're going to get them to explain everything: what we're allowed to do, what we're not; where we're allowed to do it and where we can't; why some people are allowed to do some things and others aren't; who says a priest can decide to forbid one thing and not another; and how come all priests can't agree on what's a sin and what ain't.

Take dancing, for example. In my day, dancing was forbidden in our parish but not in the next parish because there everyone was Irish and they had a different bishop than us. So the Irish and the Indians could dance, and the rest of us couldn't. So one time Jude's son got his truck out and told everyone that for fifty cents he'd drop them off at the dance hall in Big Cove and pick them up later the same night. Well, we all got up in the truck and we square danced the whole night. We had Little Maxime there with his fiddle, and Gérard-à-Joe with his kazoo, and Pierre Fou was step-dancing. By the end of the evening there wasn't an Irishman or an Indian on the dance floor, we'd filled the place up. Oh, that was a great dance! And all without committing a venial sin, too. Whereas every time I danced with Gapi at our place, I couldn't take communion the next morning. That's why people around here, they thought the Irish and the Indians were pretty lucky, because they could speak English and they had a different bishop than us. Now, our bishop was a good man, I ain't saying he wasn't. He was a saint, he was. He just didn't like dancing, is all.

There was a lot of other things he didn't like, that bishop of ours. He didn't like beer, that's for sure. That was because too many people got drunk on it in the parish, and it stayed in their stomachs and made them throw up in the churchyard after mass every morning, as soon as the Blessed Sacrament hit it. But, saint that he was, that didn't stop him from saying mass each day the Good Lord let us have. Lucky thing the Good Lord himself had a cast-iron stomach or he never would've invented such a thing as communion.

They say, too, that when he was making his rounds of conformation the bishop used to drink a bit of pop, on account of the chicken was sometimes too greasy. Well, stands to reason. It ain't every day a woman has a bishop over for dinner. She could maybe be a servant in the rectory and be used to people putting on airs, and when a bishop comes over to eat she has to put her best foot forward, so she goes out and kills her fattest hen. The bishop, he could gain twenty pounds in a single week of conformation. Didn't stop him from conforming all the young ones in the county, of course. Like I said, he was a saint. But he wasn't too fond of women, no, no one could accuse him of fooling around that way. He often said in his sermons that women was the root of all evil and you couldn't trust a one of them. All the priests say that. There was one priest who didn't even trust his own mother, so they say. Poor woman had had seventeen kids, not counting the priest, so she couldn't have been much of a threat. But a woman is always a woman, so he says. It was a woman who done the original sin in the Garden of Eaton. Her husband would've never taken that apple if she hadn't handed it to him. That's because a man is weak, you see, and he couldn't have just said no thanks. It wasn't his fault; she should never have tempted him like that and made him fall into sin. That's why after that she was punished and had to obey her husband in all things, because he's the master and the stronger of the two. It's only when he's tempted by a woman that he gets weak. Apart from then, he's the strongest.

Anyways, women can't complain, because it's their own fault that everything got off on the wrong foot. If only the first woman could've kept her wits about her and not fooled around with that damned apple from that tree. I mean, to throw away Paradise for the sake of an apple! If you ask me, if the first woman pushed her husband to do something wrong, then there must have been someone pushing her, too. It couldn't have been all her fault. I don't know any woman around here who'd trade Paradise for an apple, I don't care how nice and juicy it is. So why should the first woman be any dumber than anyone else? No, in my opinion she was pushed into it, or else it was some kind of trap, or else it had to happen so we can all earn our ticket to Heaven by the sweat of our brow. And if that's the case, I don't see why one person should get all the blame for it over another. Because what they tell us is, it doesn't matter which one of us, if we'd been either Adam or Eve we'd have done the same thing as they did. It had to happen the way it happened. So then, as I sometimes ask myself, why is it they gave us Paradise in the first place if they knew in advance we was going to screw it up? Why did they have to tempt us with Paradise at all? We didn't ask for it.

It was like we was cut out to be sinners, you see, so they had to give us something to sin about. And so it was Eve who got the ball rolling. And now women, well . . . it was the bishop himself who said it. And he's a saint, so he ought to know what he's talking about.

And then there's the meat we weren't allowed to eat on Fridays. Of course, the Irish couldn't eat it either. Fish on Friday, that was the rule. For everyone who could afford it, anyways. Wasn't a problem for us, we got more fish here on the coast than we got meat. But according to my late father, we got relatives living inland, down around Acadieville, and it seems it wasn't so easy for them to lay their hands on fish every Friday. They was farmers, and they'd kill themselves a pig for the winter. They didn't have no herring or cod down there at all. So on Fridays they'd eat just bread and molasses so they wouldn't die with salt pork on their consciences. But Gapi, he says fish on Fridays was a good thing, because it let poor fishermen sell their oysters and salmon and lobsters to the genteel folk who didn't want to give up their Lent nor their abstinence.

But what I don't understand is this: on the one hand, the Good Lord said it wasn't easy for a rich man to enter the Kingdom of Heaven, but on the other hand it seems to me that it's hard for a rich man to go anywheres else. A person of means can obey all the commandments of God and the church without too much trouble, he can pay his tithe, honour his father and his mother when they get too old to take care of themselves, buy fresh fish every Friday, go to mass every Sunday and have his own pew to sit in, and live a life of dignity and respect without having to rob or beat up his neighbour to get what he wants. A rich man can get himself a good education, too, and an educated man don't swear or curse, and he knows better than to take the Lord's name in vain. He gets used to working, too, because there's always work for rich people as long as they ain't too lazy. So, okay, you take a man who don't swear, don't steal, never misses mass, looks after his old man in his reclining years, and who ain't lazy, and you explain to me how someone like that don't go to Heaven when he kicks the bucket. He gets up to the gate without a single damned sin left on his plate. There's them who have no choice but to go to Heaven whether they want to or not — they were destined to go there since the day they was born.

Destiny. Now there's a curious thing, don't you find? What exactly is it, would you say? There's them as says a person comes into this world with his Heaven or Hell already running in his veins. If that's true then we're all in one funny kind of pickle. It wouldn't matter how hard we worked in our lifetimes . . . It may be true, for instance, that we sometimes maybe forget to keep all the commandments all the time. If we concentrate on one, we let a couple of others slip. You know, maybe it's hard to honour your father and your mother without sticking your nose into your neighbour's business; or, as it might be, you can't pay your debts and tithe without working on Sundays. Good God Almighty, for a poor person to faithfully keep all the commandments, it would be like a cripple doing somersaults on a telephone wire!

The hardest is the charity work: giving food to them as are hungry and clothes to them as haven't got none, and going into jails to sucker them as are in there. I mean, when you've spent the whole week in a prison, you hardly want to go back in again on Sunday. And why would you want to give clothes or a loaf of bread to someone who couldn't possibly need them more than you do yourself? It's not easy for a poor person to do charity or give to the church. So you end up never being sure of your own salvation, like them as are able to pay for it in cash.

Gapi, he says that if Paradise is only meant for rich folks, then he'd just as soon not go there at all. As far as he's concerned, any eternity you can buy would be too much like being down here on earth, and he's had enough of that already, thank you very much.

He can be hard, can Gapi, and when he gets riled he could just as soon set fire to Heaven using the blasted flames of Hell itself as look at you. But what I tell him is this. It's no good getting yourself all worked up about it, or trying to wiggle out of anything, or plunking yourself down in a corner and saying you ain't going nowhere. It's not like when you're dead it's all over. You got to put your feet down somewheres. You can't just stick where you are, I says, like some kind of fence post stuck between life and death, or as you might say on the border between Heaven and Hell. You've got to go to either one side or the other, and it ain't really up to you which one. It'll all be decided beforehand, because it's what you do now that counts.

Yes, yes, I know, it's not always up to you what you do, but you do have some say in it. Maybe not a lot, but some. You can always give it a shot. What I mean is, you can try to have some say. Or at least try not to do anything that's prohibited. Because what I've heard priests say is that when you do something bad it's you alone who's doing it, no one's helping you do it, which is why they say your sins are yours alone. But when you do good, it's the Good Lord who's doing it through you, and the good belongs to him. So what that means, I guess, is that whatever you do by yourself is for your eternal damnation, and if you want to do something to save your soul you got to ask God to get involved in it, if he wants to. That's why when all's said and done we're never too sure about where we stand in all of that, or how we can go about getting God to be on our side. Especially for us as hasn't got the means to do everything it says to do in the ten commandments and follow all them theological virtues and works of spiritual and corporal mercy. It's hard enough just trying to feed everyone we got living in the house and warm up their feet in our hands at night so's they'll fall asleep before daybreak. Sometimes we barely have time to drop to our knees beside our beds and try to remember our prayers.

Anyways, whenever I can't remember what comes after "Pray for us sinners and give us this day our daily bread," I say whatever comes into my head in a way so the Good Lord can understand it. Most of the time I don't say nothing, because my old washer-woman's knees won't let me stay kneeling down for too long. Usually I just end up saying I hope the Good Lord has faith in me and gives me the strength to have faith in him, amen. You won't find that prayer written up in the holy books anywhere and I wouldn't try to get away with it in church, but when it's just him and me at home, me on my knees beside the wood stove, I figure the Good Lord ain't so damned particular.

On Fortune Telling

Okay, first you shuffle the cards, then cut the deck, then make your wish. That's it. Cut it twice. Any wish you want, it's up to you. You made it? Okay, that's good. Now we're going to find out what hand life's already dealt you, and what cards it still has up its sleeve.

Right. Oh, boy!

Maybe you better take off your coat, it could get kind of warm in here. Are you comfortable? So, first, remember not to get yourself in a state, or all upset about nothing. Whatever the cards tell you will be the truth, that's for sure, only you've got to remember that the truth comes in different suits, as my father used to say. Sometimes it's hard to know what the truth is trying to tell you. Me, all I can tell you is what the cards say. Go ahead, hang your coat up on that nail over there and sit down, make yourself at home. Now, you take the little pedlar, there's a man who worries about his cards. Whenever he comes by here he always stops in to have his fortune read. And every time the cards tell him his luck is right behind him. Still, that didn't stop him from losing his job, his wife and his truck. When he complained about it, I told him, the truck, that's too bad, but a job and a wife that forced you to work as hard as you do, maybe you're lucky you lost them along the way. All he said was, if his luck was following him, it sure as hell was doing it from a safe distance.

Okay, so you, you've got the jack of diamonds following you.

The jack of diamonds, then right behind him a club with blue eyes, white face and black hair. A club and a diamond. You're going to have to make a choice. It's always tough when you come to a turning point in your life and you have to make a choice. If you want to know . . . but you can't know, can you? A person never knows ahead of time what's waiting for him down the road. But still, he can choose the thing that'll make him happy, at least. Of course, like as not he'll let it pass him by.

But to me that's not so bad as not having a choice in the first place. When your life is all staked out for you in advance, and all you can do is grab it by the coattails and hang on, well, that ain't so easy to swallow. What I say is, if a person's got no choice, it's almost like she has no freedom at all. Seems to me a person is better off making the wrong choice than living with her freedom forced on her, kind of. It's like my mother used to say, you come into this world because you don't have no choice, you're raised up to do what you're told, you get married because you have to, and then you're forced to live the rest of your life knowing all the time that you'll be in the same harness until you draw your last breath. Anyways, that's what's called having your freedom shoved down your throat, as far as I'm concerned.

Now, you take the earth, for example. You're born on it, but it ain't yours, really. Oh sure, you can tell yourself you belong here, that the earth is as much yours as anyone else's, and you can walk around on it like you own it, but sooner or later you're going to bang your head against a wall or a fence post with a sign on it that says No Trespassing! And you're forced to turn back. That's when you realize that the earth don't belong to you neither. Me, I know that Tim's house ain't my house, because Tim built it himself; and Élie's boat belongs to Élie, that makes sense to me; and Jude's truck is Jude's truck because he paid for it. But what about the earth? Who paid for it? Who made it? Who owned it first? Wasn't it the Good Lord? So how did it happen that now it belongs to this person and not that person? Who handed it down from father to son? Would the Good Lord himself have passed it on to everyone on his death bed? Oops, there I go, being sacrilegious. If I heard Gapi talking that way I'd tell him to go wash his mouth out with soap. I'd tell him the Good Lord is fair-minded and he didn't give the earth away to no one. Everyone just came and took it without so much as asking him. And then they left it to their descendants, who split it up amongst themselves piece by piece, until now no one's free to just go up and take it back from them.

Well, there's that darn jack of diamonds, still following you around. Better watch it. Better to have too much than too little. Still, keep an eye on that club. He's waiting for you at every turn in your life, that one is, every time you look up you can count on him being there. I'd watch him if I was you. All your joys and your hopes, all your happiness in life is tied up in that club. So watch out for it. Your happiness in life, the only way you'll ever get any is to keep on asking for it, you can't just sit back waiting for it to come along. So you got to take care, because one day, without saying nothing to nobody, it'll just pop back to where it came from. Life's funny that way. Everyone's out there looking for their own happiness, no mistake. So how come some of us finds it and others don't, that's what I'd like to know. There's men who never had problems with their hearts or their lungs, and there's women who never had even one miscarriage; and there's them as never had cold feet, or heard their own insides screaming at them, or their kids. I've known some of them wouldn't even know how to dig their own graves. They always had everything they ever wanted handed to them on a silver platter, that's why.

Had it all, as they say, but they never really had it all, because from what I see they never had no contentment. It ain't easy to make everyone happy: them as has nothing want something, and them as has something want more. It's hard. Anyways, what I say is that if a person can't have everything, it's just as well if he don't have too much. That way he can still dream of having something. Because, you see, the worst thing that can happen to a person, so it seems to me, is to drink when you ain't thirsty or eat when you ain't hungry or sleep when you don't want to go to sleep. That's the worst, to not want nothing more because you already got everything a person can ever have. That, to me, would be the worst, and I say, you're better off keeping yourself a bit on the thirsty side, so you still got some happiness to look forward to.

Okay, so you, you've got your happiness in life. At least it's around here somewhere. I can't see exactly what it is, whether it's gold or what, but it's somewhere between the diamond and the club. But here's a funny thing. Yep, you got your wish all right, you can thank your lucky stars for that. You got what you wished for, the exact same thing. But there's only one thing I don't get: you got your wish, but you don't know you got it. That's what's funny. Usually a person who knows what he wished for is pretty good at recognizing it when it comes along. But not you. And by the jumpin', unless what you wished for was to go to Heaven when you end your days, I could lay out these cards till I'm blue in the face and still not know what you wished for. I think you must've wished for something really rare and hard to find around these parts. Anyways, whatever it is is your business. I'm not going to ask you to tell me your wish.

Usually I get a pretty good idea of what people wished for. I never heard of Élie wishing for work, for example, nor Zelica, who's been widowed five times, wishing she could have a career. Young people, they make wishes like there's no tomorrow. They all want to be Jean Beliveau or Our Holy Father the Pope, as long as they think no one's going to laugh at them. At their age, they don't know how to be content with little bits, like dribs and drabs of happiness, that'll last for a while. No, they want it all and they want it now: money, nice clothes, trips abroad, motorcycles, Chryslers with the tops down, four doors, white-walls, foglights, fox tails, their arse ends scraping the pavement. They got big eyes, the young do. But when a person gets to the point where his life is maybe wearing a bit thin, he begins to understand that he can't have everything. At least not if he lives around here. Maybe in the States or Ontario it'd be a different story. But around here, after a person has been with someone for a certain length of time, and has already started raising a family, and has been living off of stamps for a few years, their wish-list gets a little stringier. They maybe wish they could win the bingo for once in their life, or that their kids would do better in school, or that they'd walk into a store and find a nice bit of calico or flannelette to make themselves some new clothes with. And then when you get really old, all you want is to live out your last days without stepping on anyone's toes, and not be too much of a burden when your time comes.

As for me, it feels funny to say so now, but I've only wished for one thing in my whole blessed life. Yep, the only thing I ever wanted in my life was to have a house. Oh, you can't call this shack I'm living in now a house. Water gets into it, and the cold and the wind, it rattles in the winter and drips in the summer, and it damn near falls down around your head every spring. Gapi can't shore it up no more because it leans too far to the south. I can't even bring my washtub into it because there ain't no place on the floor for me to set it down, and I sure ain't going to set it on the bed. So I have to do my laundry outside, winter and summer. Let me tell you, between Advent and Candlemas we don't change our socks or long johns all that often, no sir. I never asked for money. Just a house. And I'm not talking about a castle here, or even a bungalow, just an ordinary, run-of-the-mill, garden-variety house that I can do everything in. The laundry, the ironing, the cooking, raising the kids, everything done inside. Funny, eh? Because these days all you hear is women wanting to get out of their houses. As soon as they get everything they want in their houses, they can't wait to get out of them. Maybe that's what would've happened to me, too, how would I know? I know a person can get bored with having too much. They can get bored with feeling good, too. So what I sometimes says to Gapi, I says, any time a person gets tired of feeling too good, all she has to do is come down here and do my laundry for me, standing outside when it's five below zero, and then try to pull in my clothesline and change the clothes on it when everything's frozen stiffer than a Richibuctou ghost, and then eat a meal of warmed-over beans and pancakes, and crawl out of bed at four in the morning to stuff the wood stove with sticks and kindling. I think everyone should just live out their lives and accept their fates and then die when their time comes, that's what I think.

We have our time, and we have our life, and that's the way we have to go. It looks to me like we're destined to go that way. Someone meant things to happen a certain way. I don't know who, but it sure looks like we don't choose our life any more than we choose our final hour. There's them as calls it the book of life: they say Saint Peter has this huge book where all our lives is wrote down in advance, like, with our birth dates and death dates. And we can't go against our destiny, we can't change our final hour by so much as an inch. So maybe that book is what the cards see.

Now Gapi, he says that's all a load of BS. No one decided ahead of time what he was going to do in his life. Well, maybe for him it's not the same as for the rest of us. It's true no one can make Gapi do something he don't want to do. He's too pigheaded for that. If he says he's not going to go a certain way, I know him and he won't go that way and that's all there is to it. But I still say he's going to go when his time comes, just like everyone else. What, he thinks he won't die just because his time is up? Sorry, Gapi, but no one knows what they'll do when they come to that pass. But he says he's a free man and no one can lay a finger on him. He don't believe in destiny for a minute.

The other day he says to me, There's nothing wrote down. A man makes up his life as he goes along. Right now, he says, I'm free to go down to the shore and take a leak if I want to, at this very moment, and that don't appear in no book. That's what he said. Well, maybe it ain't wrote down in any book, but I'm not so sure that, whatever Gapi says, he's free to not take a leak when his body tells him it needs to. So I wouldn't go around making too much fun of destiny if I was him.

But you, now, you got clubs coming out your ears and you still ain't got away from that diamond. You see there, there's that jack still following you around. I think a time comes when a person has to make a decision. And it looks to me like that time has come for you. There's a decision you have to make. That's not me talking, that's the cards. It's the diamond and the club. You got your wish, you got your happiness in life, but everything here tells me that the time has come for you to make a choice. Maybe something to do with your line of work? Or your life line? Sorry I can't say it any plainer, but you know sometimes the cards is about as clear as the soapy water here in my bucket. Okay, now you got a ten of hearts turned up between the club and the diamond, and that means troubled water, afraid so. But don't take it to heart. From what I can see here you just hit the jackpot. It's like you found a treasure or something, oh my saints and stars! Maybe not a treasure like money . . . looks to me like something else, maybe a . . . jeez, it's hard to read your cards, you! Holy Mother of God the Father! If it wasn't almost sacrilegious to say so, I'd say your wish and your life's happiness were just around the corner. No, wait, that ain't right neither, by heavens, they're closer than that, and they're pretty good, too. Like I say, it looks to me like a real treasure and it's right around here somewheres . . . I'm practically sitting on it, so I am. Jesus Christ on a crutch!

Don't tell me your wish was that you could dunk your head in my wash bucket!

Well, never mind them cards. A person reads cards long enough she ends up seeing jacks and queens and kings all over the place, and she forgets the respect that's owed to you. You'd better shuffle the deck again.

Okay, first you shuffle the cards, then cut the deck, then make your wish. That's it. Cut twice. Any wish you want, it's up to you. You've made it? Okay, that's good. Now we're going to find out what hand life's already dealt you, and what cards it still has up its sleeve.

The jack of diamonds and a club. Well, I'll be damned!

On Spring

Well, Holy Mother of Christ, would you look at that for a morning. Gapi, come and look. Gapi! There's at least a dozen flocks of geese in the sky, and not a flake of snow on the roofs. Ah, nothing like filling your lungs with fresh air on a gosling morning like this to make you feel like a million bucks. It must be nearly April already. Gapi! Is March done yet? Must be. This has got to be spring, surely. Now I wish they hadn't taken all my calendars. I had one from the Irving, one from St. Joe's Oratory, and another one from the Mounties. There's always some kid comes and wants them for the pictures that's on them. Gapi, are we done with March yet? Not that he'd know, of course, he could care less about what day of the week it is or what month of the year. We're not any closer or further from death just because we got a calendar, or so he says, and we can't stop the days from passing by just by giving a name to them. Well, maybe we can't stop them, but at least we can watch them go by and know that some of them are better than others.

Far as I'm concerned, spring is the best season for us. Some say summer, but what I think is that if you want to be happy you got to be able to hope for something better than what you got. So when it's spring, you hope for summer. You look forward to mussels, clams, blueberries, warm weather and picnics at Sainte-Anne and Sainte-Marie. In August, there's really nothing to look forward to. It's not having a thing that makes a person happy, it's knowing you're going to get it. That's why I say spring is the best season.

I remember when I lived at my father's place, when my mother was still alive, we had a small bit of land about the house. Nothing grand, mind you, not a farm or a woodlot or nothing. About half a hayfield that about every five years my father would plough up. Before he could put it all into oats, my mother would run out and plant three or four rows of vegetables for a kitchen garden, and it would be us kids' job to keep the weeds out of it. And all the time we'd be weeding we'd be thinking about July when there'd be turnips and carrots, and about August, when we'd have corn on the cob. We never thought about mosquitoes and deer flies, or the crows and the hailstorms. You don't think about crows and mosquitoes in the spring, you watch the geese fly by and you fill your lungs with fresh air. And you wait.

Gapi, now, he says always waiting on something that ain't come yet makes a person go sort of soft in the head. According to him we're better off not thinking of nothing, that way we'll never get let down. He says no one'd ever be disappointed if they didn't go around counting their chickens before they hatched. I tell him you don't have to have big dreams, we're not talking about castles in the air or nothing. We're talking about looking forward to July, for crying out loud. We know July's coming, don't we? Can we not at least count on that? But he says we can't count on nothing and we shouldn't get all dreamy-eyed about things that ain't come about yet. Well, I says, there's one thing we can count on, and that's that Gapi won't change his mind just because we get a change of seasons. He puts about as much stock in springtime as he does in priests and oysters and the government. He says he don't trust no one to make his living for him. I'd say he don't even trust himself to do that, but never mind, we won't talk about that . . . It's hard when you don't have a trade and you can't get no training and there's no one there to help you pull yourself up by your bootstraps. Course, Gapi says he don't need no help from no one, but that's because he knows that even if he said he needed a hand there wouldn't be one there anyways. Makes it hard.

I ain't saying he's lazy, is Gapi, I ain't saying that. He gets up when he has work to do, I'll give him that much. When he used to come calling on me when I was living at my father's, my God, that was fifty years ago now, with his axe over his shoulder, he was no slouch at work, let me tell you. He was young and in his prime of life. He had shoulders on him like a, I don't know what, like a caribou or something. He stood up straight in them days, and his hair was black and his eyes about as blue as that sea down there. And he had teeth, too, and hair on his chest. It was spring, then, just like it is now. The geese was coming back from the south, and the gulls were so damn stupid they'd fly into the masts and get hung up in the sails. There was cones on the spruce already as big as your fist, and gum just a-dripping from the branches. The air and even the earth smelled so good in them days I don't think I'd've noticed it if Gapi had stunk to high heaven, without a word of a lie.

Anyways, the summer went by, and then came the fall, when the earth wouldn't grow nothing no more, and after that the winter, with ice in the bay and wind coming through the cracks in the walls. Couldn't do the washing without the clothes freezing on the line, and pretty soon Gapi started smelling like everyone else. But then when the spring started to come out of the icebox we all came out with it, and we got our health back. The air got all perfumy again, and Gapi, too, or just about. Smelled almost as good as he had the year before. But the next year spring came late and we had to bury our newborn. So anyways. That year it felt like summer sort of hooked right onto winter and we didn't have no April to speak of. I don't think the geese ever came back at all, and there was no mayflowers in the woods. It was like spring got squeezed out between the ice and the fireflies. No geese that year, no perfume in the woods, and Gapi didn't smell too good neither.

But that passed, as everything does. Bad times always go by in the end. They just go, like rancid butter when you spread it on a couple slices of bread. About all you can do is keep your eyes closed and wait it out. Sometimes you got to keep your eyes closed for a quite a stretch, but eventually spring comes along and brings the geese and the spruce cones with it. And it's like I says to Gapi, I says, you know how after you've fasted all through Lent, how good your baloney and hard-boiled eggs taste on Easter morning?

You could see spring as a kind of gift the Good Lord gives to poor people, just from him, because it's almost like you need to freeze your arse off all winter in order to really appreciate the sun in April; you got to be buried up to your neck in snow so you can go out with your axe and cut trenches for the spring runoff; and you got to eat a lot of warmed-over beans before you can smell the fresh air and dig yourself up some fresh carrots that've been sleeping all winter under the ground. People who have to suffer through the winter, that's who spring was made for, which is why I say spring is for old folks and the poor.

The way I see it, everyone has their own season, just like they have their own destiny and even their own time of death. When your time comes, you have to give in to it. You can moan and groan and gripe about it all you want, but it's going to happen all the same. Just like you got to live with your destiny, because once something is wrote down it can't be erased. Same thing with the seasons and the months of the year. It's bigger than you are. It's like the water and the sunshine and the smell of the woods all gets under your skin. It's as basic as finding something to eat. That's what I try to tell Gapi. Why do you think salmon swim upriver against the current? And why do geese fly back here against the wind? It's something to think about, that. What it says to me is, there's something in the land that puts you in the world, something that has your face on it and sort of moors you to this place.

Yes. I think that must be why you stay in one place: because it looks like you. A person ain't no different from a tree or an animal, you end up taking on the colour of the land that feeds you. You take them animals that live in the woods and turn white in the winter and then go dark again in the summer. They do that so hunters can't see them, they sort of blend in with the greenery or the snow. And I really do think that's why we end up looking like the earth, too.

Look at us, we got skin that's brown and a bit cracked, and the older we get the more lines we get in our face, like rows in a garden. And we get as many knots in our joints as there are on the branch of an old tree. And our feet dig into the ground as if they want to take root. We're just like the land itself, is what I'm saying.

Like the land, and like the sea, too. It's the sea's that's done us the most good and that's most saved us from misery. Yes sir, whenever the land give out on us, the sea's always been there, with its clams and its caplin. You should never bad-mouth the sea, I tells them, for it's saved us time and time again. Yes, even if the tides do come in so high in autumn they flush you out of your own kitchen, and even if the ice does carry off your dory in the spring, and even if storms out past the dunes do drown our fishermen every year. Even so, it's from the sea we come, and it's the sea that's most like us.

Our eyes are deep and blue from looking at our reflections in the sea. And from squinting for fish deep down, we got high cheekbones and eyebrows that meet in the middle. That's why we end up looking like the sea with the land bordering around it. That's what they say, anyways. They say our voice is low and kind of gravelly, and maybe they're right. And we don't talk too fast. It's true we don't talk too much, as a rule, because we don't have a whole lot to say to anybody. We don't usually go yammering on when there's people about from away. It ain't because we ain't got nothing to say. We could tell them about the sea, and the land, and about ourselves and all. But most of the time we just ask them about their families, or their work. And after that, well . . . it ain't all that easy, talking with a gravelly voice.

It's probably because we've breathed in too much salt from the water, and it's got stuck in our throats, and the winds coming down from the northeast have broadened our foreheads, and the beach pebbles have hardened the soles of our feet. And the gulls' moaning in the southeasterlies, with the groaning of the waves that keep crashing away at the shoreline at night, have got stuck in our ears, and that's why we don't talk too fast and we sort of let our voices trail off, or so they say.

Anyways, it's better for a person to accept himself for what he is and not go around talking and walking like someone he ain't. When you've been walking the rows of red soil for a couple of centuries, you and your ancestors, or over beach pebbles and shells, you ain't going to be soft in the legs, are you, and there won't be much of a spring in your step. And when you have to spend your life facing into the wind at sea, you ain't likely to have nice soft white skin. And how are you going to be a smooth-talking big shot when your throat and your lungs are all clogged with sea salt? No, a person's got to look like the land that put him here in the first place, and raised him, and keeps him moored to his home dock, and maybe what keeps him pining a bit, too. But not in the spring, when everything wakes up. And that's what reminds you of . . .

It's funny, but the spring always makes me want to get up and go, to whistle and walk faster than I usually do; but it also makes me pine for something, too. I don't know how to describe it. It's like I had a cork or something stuck right here, between my heart and my wishbone, or some cotton batten around my lungs. It ain't heartache, nothing like that, it's more like a longing, not a longing for anyone or anything, it's just . . . like a longing for the sun that comes from way back when.

The snow used to start melting in March, right about the middle of Lent. Some people's kids used to give up sugar or chocolate for Lent, but us kids, when we wanted to do the same thing, we used to save an orange from Christmas and set it up on top of the cupboard until Easter, for our penance. And then on Holy Saturday, no sooner did the angelus start ringing than we'd jump for that orange. Well, it was always rotten by that time. We'd lost an orange, but we'd kept our Lent and we didn't mind. And then in April we'd go out and collect tadpoles from the cricks, we used to call them figure-eights, and we put them in jars and watch them turn into frogs, and then we let them go. In May we used to walk three miles every night to church, for Mary's Month. We didn't have to go, but our route took us across the baseball diamond, and we'd stop for a bit and watch the game. Then in June there'd be rhubarb in the garden next door, and all the women would be out planting and weeding and calling out to each other from fence to fence. It's funny, but every spring it comes back to me, all that, and it kind of makes me sad.

Sad, but not sad sad, if you know what I mean, just kind of like . . . Okay, let's say you go out onto your porch one morning in the spring, and you see a bunch of geese heading up from the water behind your father's place where you was born and where you grew up. And there's a drop of water hanging from the tip of every tree branch, and you hear it hit the snow, and it runs down a rivulet to the shore and gets swallowed up by the sea. Then you smell the clover starting to come up in the fields, and the ice floating down the river. And then there's the gulls crying after the geese, and more geese coming up from the water . . .

And suddenly you don't know where you are any more. You start hearing the figure-eights calling you, and the Month of Mary songs, and the ice cracking out in the bay. It's like your whole life is gathered up in your veins, and all of a sudden you can't tell the gulls' cries from your neighbours calling out to each other. It's like all your memories come flooding in on you all at once just from seeing them geese come back at the start of spring. All your memories, all your hopes, all your sadness, and you feel like whistling and skipping around . . . but you don't, of course, because you got this cork stuck right here, and a big wad of cotton batten wrapped around your lungs.

Well, one of these days maybe we'll get us a spring, a real spring, dripping water all over and filling our noses with that musky perfume, and flocks of geese filling up the sky as far as the eye can see, and there won't be no more sadness, just a real feeling of joy in your throat and on your skin, a real spring that just goes on and on, and lasts and lasts until . . . well, that'd be Heaven, I guess, and it won't happen until we're all dead and gone to Paradise. I think I'll go down to the Saint's place, see if she don't have a spare calendar.

On the Resurrection

You take Gapi now, he don't believe that the Good Lord was resurrected on Easter morning. He says he couldn't have been. When a man's dead he's dead, he says, and that's the end of it. Well, I says, maybe a man, but the Good Lord ain't a man. He ain't? says Gapi? Well, if he ain't a man, then how come he was dead? That's when I tell him to stop his infernal blastpheming.

How come he was dead! What they tell us is, he had to be dead so he could come back to life. But why did he have to come back to life? Was it just so's he could stay with us forever? Well, I can see that he'd want to stay here with us, but . . . well, no, I can't see that neither. Not someone as dead set on salvation as the Good Lord must have been . . ., I can't for the life of me see why he'd want to keep hanging around here. If it were me, I'd . . . yes, well, it weren't me, were it?

I'd never be in his shoes, and I guess none of us ever will be. Least of all La Sagouine. All that religious mumbo-jumbo, I ain't cut out for it. I can't see me spending my life surrounded by angels, and popes, and cardinals, and holy seas, I don't think I'd find it all that comfortable. And with a job like that a person can't just rest on his laurels, you know, you got to go out and do the work, too. And to do the Lord's work would be a job and a half, I'm telling you. Specially these days. Maybe back then it was still tit for tat, but trying to run the world today, to be a fisher of modern men, except for our priest I can't see anyone but the Good Lord taking that one on, no sir.

I ain't saying the Good Lord don't know his own business, I ain't saying that. I'm sure he does know his business. He knows that if the Rockinfellers and the Rock 'n' Rollers are running the world it's for his greater glory and our greater good. Who knows what's good for us and what ain't? God knows we don't. We don't even understand the idea behind the tides coming up and flooding us out of our kitchens, which don't mean a lot because we don't even understand why it ain't such a good idea. It may well be that without the high tides one year we wouldn't get the caplin the next year. And maybe if it wasn't for recessions or what they call economic turndowns, we wouldn't get no food banks or pogey cheques. And of course we wouldn't get no widows' pension if it wasn't for our husbands being killed in the war, would we? So that's a lot to think about if you're going to run the world. No wonder the Good Lord sometimes must just be pulling his hair out of his head, the poor devil. There must be days when he asks himself why he ever made the world in the first place. Because he could just as easily not've made it at all, right? Or else he could've made it different from what it is.

That's what Gapi was saying the other day, anyways, he says, if God had to make the world, he sure as hell didn't have to make it like he did. What on earth was he thinking when he made potato beetles, for example, or when he gave wings to crows? Or why on earth would he give us eighty-mile-an-hour winds on the same day have gives us seventy-foot waves? I don't know what kind of world Gapi would've given us. I honestly don't know.

What kind of world would any of us have made in his place? If it's true that we're all going to come back to life, then we can make it any way we like. Just like the Creator did when he first made it after his own image and likeness. For me, if I was to make it after my own image it wouldn't be so bad. But after my own likeness . . . I don't know, if the resurrected world looked anything like what I got here in my pail it'd hardly be worth the trouble of carrying it up from the tomb. They carried him up from the tomb, though, after three days . . . Take them longer than three days to get me up again, I can tell you that. I'd have to wait until the end of time, I would, until after the Last Judgment was over and done with. Then I'd have about as much time ahead of me as I already spent. I don't know anyone that has to stick around after his Last Judgment. Apart from the Saint, that is, who fancies herself a cut above the rest of us. Well, when they haul her up in front of the choir of angels and start reeling off the list of all her past sins, I'll bet a dollar to a donut she won't be feeling all that saintly no more. Neither will I, come to that. When I look ahead to that day I kind of wish I'd gone in for being a nun.

I kind of like the idea of being brought back to life when the last strumpet has sounded. But here's a question for you: does that mean that when you come back you'll be the same age as you was when you departed? If I die when I'm ninety years old, am I going to have to drag them ninety years around with me for all eternity? And the Humpback, will he still have his hump? And what about old Monique's fish eye? What they say is we won't care, we'll be perfectly happy. But to be perfectly happy they'd have to give Monique her eye back, and give the Hunchback a new body. Me, they'd have to give my muscles a good rub-down and drain the water out of my knees. And as for Gapi, well, forget it, it'd take a whole regiment of archangels to get him back on his feet. He won't settle for two arms and thirty-six teeth, not him, I know him too well for that: they'd have to give him something nobody ever saw before, or something bigger than whatever everyone else got. He's awful bilious, is Gapi. I feel sorry for whoever gets the job of resurrecting him.

Anyways, they'll have to bring him back to life same as the

others, I guess. They can't very well leave him lying there in the churchyard when everyone else is risen from the dead and on their way rejoicing, can they? Everyone has to rise up on Judgment Day; we all have to go through the judging and then through the rising up, young and old, rich and poor alike. Except with the poor you won't see a big difference; they couldn't look much worse than they did when they was alive, because they couldn't raise them up any poorer dead than they was before. It's different for the rich; for them it's not entirely clear that the resurrection'll be a good thing. Suddenly there's Dominique-à-David stepping stark naked out of his tomb without even a hip pocket to put his wallet in, and what good's a new life to Dominique if he ain't got his wallet with him? And if there's no more judgments after the Last Judgment, what are they going to do with all the judges and the lawyers? And what about the doctors, if there ain't going to be no more sick people? Come to that, what're they going to do with me? I'm pretty sure they won't be needing no one to wash floors up there in Kingdom Come. Which I don't mind, I'll get a chance to rest my weary bones.

I'll be able to rest them for a long time: all eternity. We don't have nothing down here that even comes close to eternity. At the mission there was a priest from away, and he told us that if a bird just brushed his wing on a rock once every hundred years, by the time that rock was all wore away eternity would just be getting started. He couldn't have meant a bird from around here, though. All the birds I know would be long dead before that rock wore away. He also told us, this missioner, that there was no chance of being bored stiff in eternity, because we'd be spending all our time listening to the songs of skylarks and such, and smelling the flowers of Paradise. That's what he said, anyways, and he was a priest, so you'd think he'd know. He also said that we'd all be given a white dress to wear and a candle. That's when Gapi flat out said no. And no matter how much I tried to tell him he could keep his overalls on under his dress if he liked, he wouldn't budge. He'd rather take a pass on resurrecting, thank you very much.

Well, that's Gapi for you. You can see he don't have a real good grasp on the mysteries. I says to him, I says, make an effort, try to understand. But it ain't all that easy when we're not taught to understand the resurrection. Oh sure, for priests and lawyers it's all kid's stuff. But for the rest of us . . . All they taught us was that a mystery was a truth that we had to believe whether we understood it or not. Well, you try understanding something once you've been told a thing like that! I understand that I'm going to die, and that my body'll go to the cemetery, and that my soul'll either go to Purgatory or Paradise, depending. But me, La Sagouine, where'll I be all that time? They say that at the resurrection my soul and my body will be reunited, and I'll go back to being the person I was before I died. But don't forget, that's at the Last Judgment, way at the other end of time. Do I have to stay split in two like that until the end of time? And how do I know that time won't get it into its head to come to an end before that? What'll happen to me in the meantime? Anyways, that's the kind of idea that's been crawling around in my head lately, like I got ants in the brain or something.

I got lots of other ideas swarming through my head, always have. Mostly about the resurrection and eternity. Like, when they tell me it was God who made us, and who made the world and who made all the things that have been in the world since then, I always want to know who it was who made God. Who made God? they say. Well, no one made God. He made himself. He made himself all by himself, in eternity. So all during eternity God was there, by himself? Well, not exactly by himself: there was three of him, three persons in one. Good thing too, because they could keep themselves company so they wouldn't get bored. So no matter how far back you trace your ancestry, God was there before that? Yes. Okay, so then you ask yourself, what was there before God was there? And the answer is: God was there. So before God came along, he was already there. That's what eternity is, they say.

Right. Well, I know the world didn't make itself by itself, there must have been someone who made it up out of nothing. And that must have been the Good Lord. But how was it that there was no one around to make him up out of nothing? There's times I tell myself it's just as hard for God to make himself up out of bugger-all as it is for the world to make itself up by itself. But there I go talking like Gapi, being sacrilegious against the whole Trinity United.

I believe in God the Father Almighty, maker of Heaven and earth, and in his only son our Lord Jesus Christ, forgotten by the Holy Spirit . . . The Holy Spirit, now, he was the one who turned himself into a firefly at the Pentecostal and landed on the heads of the apostles to bring them the gift of tongues, so's they could all speak different languages. Now, the apostles, they weren't but a bunch of poor fisher folk no different from us, and they come out of the Pentecostal with their heads a-swimming and suddenly found themselves speaking seven different languages, if you can believe it, something like Marguerite Michaud, who started the library up to Fredericton. So when you take a bunch of fishermen and get them speaking seven different languages, you got yourself a mystery don't matter what kind of fish they catch. You can't very well explain it, you just got to believe it, because it was revealed by God.

That's a lot of stuff to understand for a bunch of poor people who never went to school for too long but who all the same want to know in advance what to expect when they get to the Other Side. Because if we could just have a tiny smidgen of an idea of what's in the next world, we can maybe plan better for the trip, and not arrive there like a bunch of ninnies who don't know nothing about nothing. We don't want to embarrass God and the Holy Virgin and all the rest of them whenever we return to Paradise at the end of time. We want to get there on an equal footing with everyone else. That's why we'd like to have a religion with a few fewer mysteries and a bit more bread to bite into on Easter morning.

Okay, that's enough thinking about that, it makes my head swim, like when I'm crossing the railroad bridge and I look down between the ties and see the water.

Gapi says I'm just getting myself all worked up over nothing. He says that's the kind of thinking that'll end a person up in Saint John. If you think too much about death all the time, he says, you're going to bring it on early. I tell him it ain't death I think about, it's what comes after. Well, he says, what comes after death is just death. And I tell him to stop being sacrilegious.

There's only the one thing we know for dead certain and that's that we're all going to pass on some day. We don't know where we're going to pass on to, but we're going to pass through something. And if we come out the other side it's because we was resurrected. And then, so it seems, we'll have everything we could ever want. Just thinking about it makes most of the water in my knees come up into my mouth. An eternity to remake the world any way you want! To hold it in your hands, shape it, smooth it off, tart it up a bit, and . . . can't you just see it? A whole eternity just for you and your resurrection by yourself! No, not just for yourself. Not all alone. With God. No, wait, not just with you and God, either: with everyone.

Joséphine, and Séraphine, and Pierre-à-Tom, and Élie; and Maxime with his fiddle; and Pierre the Fool, it'll be good to see him again. And probably Laurette-à-Johnny'll be there, and Johnny, too, who's dead, but even so. I always managed to get my way with Laurette, but not with the Saint. Once she gets to the Other Side it'll be nothing but vespers and supplications blessings from the Holy Sacrament for at least an eternity, maybe more if she takes it into her head to start in on novenas for the Stations of the Cross. If you think she's been sucking up to the Good Lord all her life down here, imagine what she'll be like when she sees him face to face! No, I don't count on seeing the Saint up there. I still mind the day she stole a pot of stew off my own doorstep. She won't be bringing that into Paradise, not her. But if she still has it she can damn well take it with her somewhere else . . . Ah, now, maybe it ain't lucky to wish a person to go to Hell for a pot of stew. And I'm pretty sure it ain't Christian. I'm going to go up to her and tell her she has to make a choice: she can't get into Heaven with my stew. And she has to give the Crotch back her two poutine râpée, and the fox tail she took off of Noume's Ford to put around her neck. And while we're at it, Noume can give back the beer he took from Élie, and Élie'll have to return Gapi's scythe and rake . . . And I guess I better not keep Séraphine's shoes, neither, or them Eaton's catalogues I borrowed from the Saint's place. I think everyone had best get their affairs put in order. The Saint, now, if she'd just stop scheming and sticking her nose in other people's business, I'd let her in. Give her fair warning: don't go starting no trouble. Now I got to hope that Gapi don't get it into his head not to come. I better go and talk to him right away.

There's things you can't put off getting straightened out. You can wait a whole year before replacing the duckweed around your shack, or reshingling your roof. And likewise there's no big rush to clean out the inside of the cupboard or hang the blankets on the clothesline to air out. But a person who puts off his own salvation might find himself turning up late for the resurrection. Me, I missed out on a few things in my time, but I ain't going to miss out on this one, no sir. And I'm going to tell Gapi as much. He don't want to believe that the Good Lord resurrected himself on Easter morning? Well, fine and good, he can believe it or not believe it, don't matter to me. But get this into your thick skull, I'm going to tell him: don't for a second think I'm going to lift you up from your grave on Judgment Day and get you resurrected in spite of yourself. You better be ready to spend all of eternity on your own, and it's probably going to last a lot longer than you think. That's what I'm going to tell him.

I'm going to tell him straight to his face, this very minute.

On the Census

Yeah, well, they came down here and did the census. We was all censused, no problem. They censused Gapi, and they incensed the Saint, and they censored me, too. It was a pretty big deal, take my word for it without a word of a lie. When they do a census like that, they got to cense everyone, even the chickens and pigs. We ain't got no chicken coop or pigsty at our place, so they censused the cats. They rummage around in your cupboard, too, and measure the size of your house. They even count the damn shingles on your roof. When they asked Gapi if they could see his bank book he told them they could go piss up a rope. He can't keep a civil tongue in his head, that man can't.

They ask you all kinds of questions. Some of them are hard to answer. What's your name? What names were you baptized with? Who's your father? What was your mother's maiden name? What did you have when you were last sick? When was it you were born? How many children dead? How many living? How much money do you make a year?

In Gapi's opinion, they were sticking their noses a bit too deep into his business, like when they asked him what his father did before he died, he looked right at them and said, "Before he died?" he says, "well, he stretched out his legs and went, 'Arghhh!'"

Like I say, they can ask some damn fool questions.

What it comes down to is, when you get censused you got to

remember everything that happened to you your whole damn life. It's worse than confession, for Christ's sake! They wanted to know how much we spend on flour in a year. In a year, no less! Now, is there anyone on God's green earth can tell you exactly how much money they spend in a year? We buy our flour by the pound, one small bag at a time, and whenever we run out, or when we got enough dough to pay for it, or more likely when they'll give it to us on credit, we go out and get some more. And we use it to make bread with, or pancakes, not account books, which is what Gapi told the censors. And we don't keep tabs on every damn clam or quahog we sell, neither. All's we could tell the census was that we fish so we can sell, we sell so we can buy, and we buy so we can eat. And if we're lucky, at the end of the year we've put about the same amount of fish in our bellies as we fished out of the bay. Down here, that's what we call economics.

And they can ask even harder questions than that, too. Like when they asked the Crotch to explain what she did for a living, or when they asked Boy the names of all his children. Oh, they can come up with some real head-scratchers!

Then they ask you what's your religious persuasion. Well, so you're all ready to answer that one and then you think, Okay, wait a minute, now. There's one or two things that need to get explained first. It ain't a simple matter of was you dipped in the font and conformed by the archbishop himself when he came around on his tour. They want to know who's the patron saint of your home parish. Well, by home parish do they mean the one where you do your Easter duties on Trinity Sundays, or the one where your children was baptized, or what? What's a home parish? We didn't want them to think we was a bunch of Commies down here, so we just told them we was all Christians.

And that ain't the end of it, because the hardest question of all was still on their list. What's your nationality? Not even Gapi

knew the answer to that one. Your citizenship and your nationality. Well, it's hard to say.

We live in America, but we ain't Americans. The Americans
all work in stores in the States, and they come up here for their
summer vacations and walk around wearing white shorts and
speaking English. And they're all rich, them Americans, whereas
we ain't. We live in Canada, so I guess that makes us Canadians.
But that don't sound right, neither, because there's the Dysarts
and the Carrolls and the Joneses who ain't the same as us, and
they all live in Canada, too, so if they're Canadians then I guess
we can't be. Because they're English, and we ain't. We're French,
you see.

No, we're not really French, neither, that's not what I meant
by that. When you say you're French it means you come from
France. And we're less French from France than we are Americans. So we're more like French Canadians, is how they put it
to us.

Well, no, we ain't that, neither, because French Canadians,
that's people who live in Quebec. They used to call themselves
Canadiens, but now they're all Québécois. So how can we be
Québécois if we don't live in Quebec? Well, for the love of all
that's holy, where the hell do we live, then?

We live in Acadia, so we been told, and that means we're
Acadians. So that's what we put down under Nationality: Acadian. Because if there's one thing we know for sure, there ain't
nobody else with that name. But the censors, they didn't want to
write that on their list, because they said there's no such country
as Acadia, and so Acadian can't be a nationality. There's no such
place in their jogger-free books.

So after that we didn't know what else to tell them, so we just
told them to give us whatever nationality they wanted. In the end
I think they lumped us in with the Natives.

It ain't easy to make a life for yourself when you don't even have your own country to live it in, and you can't tell nobody what nationality you are. You end up not having the faintest idea who you are any more. You feel like kind of a fifth wheel, you know what I mean? Like nobody wants you around. It ain't them that makes you feel that way. They tell you you're a bond-ified citizen, but they can't tell you a citizen of what. You're part of a country, maybe, but you have no place in it. So sooner or later you got to leave to go find yourself a place, one of us after another.

I hear the Saint's boy Arthur has sent for his mother. Yeah, he went up to Montreal last fall, and it looks like he found a job there in a shop making plastic flowers, and now he's sent money for his mama to go up and live with him. Well, you can just bet she's going to doll herself up something fierce, with that feather hat she got from the doctor's wife and the fox tail she stole off of Noume's Ford. She'll wear them Montreal sidewalks down to pebbles strutting up and down them like the Queen of Sheba. And she'll light her candles in St. Joe's Oratory, and put a dollar one at the foot of Brother André's heart.

Well, at least we'll have some peace around here, for a time anyways. Depends on how long she stays up there. Gapi, he says we've seen the end of her. That Gapi! What's he mean by that? He's always got to take a negative view of things.

He also says that Laurette-à-Johnny is going to move down to the States and that Jos-à-Polyte is ready to take his family down to warmer climes. He says he heard it over to the Moose's place. Looks like before long we won't have a blessed neighbour to help us put our boat in the water. Ah, the times sure are a-changing, as the song says, and we could be seeing another bunch of census takers coming down here again, measuring everything up, screw-ing everything up, and shipping us all down south.

It ain't like it ain't happened before, getting shipped down south, and that time we ended up in Louisiana. We don't want to go through all that again, do we? Don't they think once was enough? My father used to say his grandfather could remember when it happened, the Expulsion, and evenings he'd tell stories about what they went through in them days. They walked through the bush for weeks and months to get back here, because they wanted a country of their own, just like we do. They wanted a piece of land that would be theirs, where people spoke their language and nobody called them names. That's why they came back here, to their own country, to live on their own land. That's what they did. They were the ancestors of my late father. Well, they didn't exactly get their old land back; the English owned it all. All's that was left for them was to take their axes and cut down trees and start to rebuild. They rebuilt their cabins and rebuilt their lives, too, on the land of their forefathers, even though during the Expulsion they lost the deeds to it along with their nationality.

Couldn't have been easy, being deported like that and not to think you lost something important along the way. Takes a lot out of you, a trip like that. No wonder they told stories about it afterwards, stories with a lot of nice names into them, like Evangeline and the Blessed Canadian Martyrs. You get called a heroic and martyred people and you're practically nailed up there on the cross with the Good Lord himself, and people'd come down from the cathedral in L'Assomption and the Monument of Recognition on purpose just to tell us about it in the church basement. They'd tell us all about Evangeline and Ave-Marie-Stella, and a nice story it was, too, about Marie-Stella and Evangeline. But I still preferred the stories my late father used to tell.

There's the one about Pierre-à-Pierre-à-Pierrot, who dressed himself up like a woman, imagine that, and saved himself by climbing up a tree and jumping from branch to branch like a monkey so's not to be seen by the Natives or the English who were looking out for him in the bush. He was out getting help for the others who were hiding in a root cellar, an empty one at that. And there's the one about Captain Belliveau, who was one of the prisoners being deported when he threw all the English overboard and took control of the ship. Well, that was one ship that never saw the Louisiana coast, I'll tell you. Captain Belliveau took it somewhere up north, according to my father, and the English never saw it again. They were pretty tough customers, were our ancestors, they wasn't easy to haul in. But they wasn't the real heroes and martyrs. No, the real heroes and martyrs was Evangeline and Marie-Stella.

Yes sir, we come from a long line of holy martyrs, so they tell us. To listen to them, we were lucky we were deported like that. Well, if that's true then we were pretty damn lucky. First of all, according to them, about half of them that was forced onto the British ships came back. Then, of them as came back, about half were lucky enough to make it through the first winter. That was more than two hundred years ago now, and there's still a goodly number of us left alive. Like the English themselves tell us, how many races are there who wouldn't've just sunk to the bottom after being caught in a storm like that? You can count yourselves good and lucky, they told us. I guess when they put it like that, yes, we was lucky.

Well, it's two hundred years later and we're still here. Still working our weedy fields, still fishing for clams and oysters and caplin, still trying to make ends meet and not to die before we pass away. Don't kick the bucket until it's full, is what I always say. And make sure your grave is dug in holy ground if you want to take your rightful place in Paradise. As for the rest, well, for us there ain't no rest.

But it's enough, little though it be, and we'd like to hang on to it for a spell, if that's okay. We also wouldn't mind it if we could go on living in our shacks and on our land for a little while, yet. Not that it's real good land, of course, more like what they call abandoned land that don't belong to nobody else that our ancestors built on when they came back and didn't want to make a big fuss and upsettle anyone. We sort of plan on sticking around for a few more generations without getting in anyone's way. We don't live big, we've never been the kind of people to lay back and take life easy. That ain't us. We're happy just to keep going on the way we have been, splitting kindling and cutting holes in the ice to fish caplin in the winter, and in the spring waiting for the geese to come back and let us know that the sap's running in the trees and our lungs'll soon be filled up with fresh air for the summer. And then you got your blueberries and string beans in July, and your corn on the cob in August, and then comes autumn . . .

This coming autumn the Saint will be at her son's place in Montreal. And Laurette'll also have flown the coop. And Jos-à-Polyte, and the Moose, and . . . and I guess me and Gapi, too, we'll soon enough have to take our turn at leaving. They've gone and confiscated all the land along the coast, so they tell us, because it ain't, I don't know, eugenic or something, it's like a drain on the country's economy. I don't know where we're going to end up, Gapi and me. It ain't like we got a son in Montreal or kin in the States to take us in, that's for sure. But, like I told Gapi, we can't stay here by ourselves, neither, being a drain on the country.

Gapi, he ain't convinced that we're screwing up their economy. The way he sees it, there's more people been mistreated by the country than country that's been beat down by people. And if a piece of land can't support us, then it sure as hell won't support whoever else they put on it after they take us off it. It ain't right, he says, shifting people from one place to another, and then . . . Well, I just tell him to keep his opinions to himself and quit his bellyaching. Pack up your overalls and your change of long johns and get yourself ready to move. That's right, I says, we got to get ourselves ready for the next Expulsion, because this time I don't know when we're ever going to make it back. If we ever do . . . if we're ever going to have a country of our own, once and for all, where we can plant our beans again and stuff duckweed around our cabins to keep the wind out. I don't know if . . . I just don't know.

We got nothing for them to censor, them census-takers. That's what I told them. Gapi, too, he told them the same thing. We got no land of our own, we can't say what religion we are, we don't know what our nationality is. We don't think we have one. We're lucky to be still alive, they tell us, and I guess they're right. We're still alive. So they tell us. But if we wasn't I doubt they or anyone else'd notice. Not even the census-takers. When you get to the point where a people can't name their religion, or their race, or their country, or their land, and they don't even know what language they speak, well then, I'd say you got a people that don't even know what kind of people they are. I'd say you got a people that don't know nothing about nothing.

That's what I'm going to say to the government: I don't know nothing no more, I don't belong to nothing, maybe I even am nothing. But I'm still alive and kicking. As far as I know my name's still La Sagouine, and with a handle like that they ain't going to take me for one of them census-takers or a doctor's wife. They're going to have to look me in the eye when they see me walking right along beside them down the Post Road.

On Death

I live down there, but that ain't where I was born. I was born higher up, before the war. Not this last war, the first war. I know they say it wasn't the first war, that there was other wars before that one, and I guess they're right. But I didn't know about them. I only know about two wars, but that's enough to give you some idea of what war is. A small idea, anyways. Yes, I'll have another splash of tea, if you still got some left.

Yep, La Sagouine, that's what they calls me. You know, I don't believe if my own dead mother was alive, God bless her soul, she'd be able to recall what name I was baptized under. I must have had one at one time. I mean, I was dipped in the font like everyone else, sure as I'm sitting here. Somebody held me up, and I was given a godmother and a godfather, and they was all from around here. My whole family was, according to my father. Dipped and baptized and wrapped up in my christening gown, went through the whole shooting match before I even had my eyes open, as you might say. We're all the same at that age, eh? It ain't till later that . . . You better drink up your tea while it's still hot. It'll settle your stomach and your kidleys. That's where it gets to me, especially at night, pain like you wouldn't believe. Right here, in the small of my back. It's as if my insides was all twisted up and they're trying to get untwisted, like a spring or something. Happens every night, brought by the Good Lord himself.

Well, maybe it ain't the Good Lord that brings on the night, or the pain . . . When Gapi starts talking like that I tell him to zip it up. Don't talk like that, I says to him. The Good Lord knows his business. Gapi says it ain't right, that if the Good Lord was as good as everyone says he is, he wouldn't allow such pain and suffering in the world for no good reason. Put a lid on it, I tells him. We don't want to start getting blastphemous, for crying out loud. If we've got to put up with evil in the world it's probably because of something we did. It's our own fault . . . Gapi says that the evil that's done in the world isn't real evil, it's just people playing little tricks on God, for laughs, and the Good Lord don't need to get all squirrelly about it and treat us like a bunch of sinners looking around to make trouble for the sake of trouble.

At night is when it hits me, right in the stomach and at the base of my spine. I set out to see the doctor in town about it a couple of times, but I never made up my mind to go in . . . Laurette, she went and told everyone that I didn't see him because when I got into town I always found something better to do than hang around in the hospital all day. She should talk. After Johnny died she had her hair frizzed and started really playing at being a widow. A hussy, more like, and it didn't start when Johnny died, neither. Anyways, each to his own, eh? No, I just couldn't bring myself to go in. Once the doctor says you got a certain condition, then you're stuck with it whether you got it or not. I ain't afraid of being sick, I just don't want the sickness that never gets better.

Once you're dead, you're dead for a long time. Some people are afraid of dying, but I ain't. I figure a twitch in the guts and it's all over. I been through worse in my life, I can get through that. No, it ain't death, it's what comes after that scares the bejesus out of me. Like, is it true what it says in the cataclysm books about your Purgatory and your Limbo and your Hell freezing over? Gapi, he says if the Good Lord is really good . . . But I tell him

I don't want to hear no more of his nonsense. He says there can't be no Hell down below for poor people because we're already in it up here.

When Gapi and me got married we went to the priest and asked him to tie the knot for us, but he refused. Because of our relations. I can't marry you, he says, because you're related too close to each other. Well, it's true we come from a close-knit family, my late father and Gapi's mother was brother and sister. That makes us first cousins, the priest told us, and according to the law covering marriages, first cousins can't get married, at least not to each other. Well, I looks at Gapi and he looks at me, and then he says to me, if it's all the same to you we can go get married by the minister. So that's what we did, we went to the minister's, and he didn't have no problem with it, and so we left his place man and wife. Two weeks later, I think it was, Gapi was coming in with his catch and I went down to the dock to meet him, and we ran into Father Nap, who at the time was the priest at Sainte-Marie.

So Father Nap, he says to us, he says, "Look, you two, you know damn well you're not really married. If you come with me maybe I can fix it up."

Well, I looks at Gapi and Gapi looks at me, and Gapi says, "If we was first cousins last week, we're first cousins this week, too. What do we need to go with you for?"

And the priest, he says, keeping his hat on, "Come on, it won't take a minute, come on up to the rectory and I'll marry you in the church, it'll be over in two shakes."

So Gapi looks at me and I looks at Gapi, and Gapi says, "Well, if you say so . . ."

So we follow Father Nap up to the rectory, and he confesses us, marries us and blesses us, and he even turns down the dollar that Gapi was going to fork over. There, Gapi says, we're married twice, that must count for something. This time it was a real

137

wedding, with a ring and everything, a nice big one made out of pure limitation gold. Lost it on the church steps, as I recall. Anyways, it's like they says, when you got twelve kids you don't need no wedding ring.

Yep, twelve kids. We was able to save three of them; the other nine died when they was still in diapers. You got to remember that in them days when I was raising children we didn't even put duckweed around the houses, and all we had to burn was green wood and kindling. And if that wasn't enough, all nine of them was born between All Saints' and spring thaw. The three that was born in raspberry season made it okay. Yes, it was your own mother that delivered them, yes it was. She was a saint, your mother was, a real fine woman, yes, that's right, and I don't doubt for a minute she's looking down on us from Heaven as we're sitting here. She supplied everything: diapers, blankets, swaddling clothes, even the hot water. A real fine woman. If there'd been more women like her I might not have lost the other nine. Well anyways, as I says to Gapi, at least I ain't worried about them, they're all there together in the cemetery. I ain't worried about them at all, I know they're all right, they weren't here long enough to do anything bad. I barely had time to get them baptized.

I go into town whenever I get my government cheque. But I don't go in them houses no more, in fact I walk way out of my way so's I don't pass in front of them. Rosie called after me the other day, but I pretended not to hear her. And then I yelled back at her that she could go straight to Hell for all I cared. And she says, Come on over here, I want to talk to you. And I say, You got any men in there? And she says, No, I'm damn well alone. All right, I says, let me come and have a look. Well, where's the sense in living like she still does at her age, that's what I want to know, and death written all over her face? It's like I says to the judge, I says, I made a promise to Saint Anne and I intend to keep it. And now the judge and me are like that.

Thanks, wish I could make a cup of tea this good. Coats the lungs, is what it does. It's good tea leaves that does it, you're right, it's in the leaves. You can almost see your whole life in them. I guess I'll go see the doctor, one of these days. Long as I'm at it I might as well see the best. A specialist in them parts down there, because that's where the pain is. The worst of it is always down there, ain't it, coming into this world as well as leaving it. And there's not a long enough time in between, you can take that from La Sagouine. Seems like just yesterday I was picking blueberries down to the bog and my grandmother was saying to me, Pick only the real ripe ones, she says. Leave the others for seeds. And don't touch nothing white.

Don't touch nothing white, I thought to myself. Is that why we wore a white veil at our first communion, then? Of course, I was just young, but it makes you wonder, don't it. You forget after a while, you don't think about such things no more. You try to make ends meet, and you stitch them together so the seams don't show too much. But they always show once you've torn your skirt, just as well not to think about it after that. You think you can give up on thinking altogether, but there's too much to not think about, that's the problem. There's the dances and the homebrew and then the kids that couldn't be saved, and the squabbles with the neighbours, and baloney on Fridays, and mass on Sundays, which you skip because you only got a beat-up old hat to put on your head and you don't want no one to make fun of you. All my life it's been too much. The Good Lord can be as good as he likes, but . . .

The priests tell us he forgives us all our sins because he's infinitely good. As long as you're sorry you done them, I guess, which seems fair enough. As I says to Gapi, if you want to be forgiven for your sins, then you got to be sorry you done them and you'll try hard not to do them again. So does that mean if you had your life to live over you'd . . .? Yes, I guess it does, if you had your life to live over you'd live it different, that's it in a nutshell right there.

It's hard, though, ain't it, because a person don't always have a choice. If my kids'd wanted for nothing like some other people's kids then I wouldn't have had to move into town to work on Main Street or wait for ships to come in from the old countries. I wouldn't have had to do that. "You could've told me what you done with Dan's boy on the wharf down to Saint-Norbert," Gapi says to me once. "You could've told me about it before we was married," he says. Oh sure, I could've told him all right. But when? When did I have time? Because it happened with him like it happened with Dan's boy and I never had time to tell nobody nothing. And what would've been the good of telling him after-wards, eh? It just would've made him feel bad, and anyways, it was too late. Don't matter if you feel bad about something, once a thing's done it's done.

The only way to get around that is to regret doing something before you do it. I ain't saying it's easy. In my opinion, the worst sins are the ones you do when you know you're doing something wrong and you go ahead and do it anyways. You're free to make your choice. I mean, a person's always free to do something or not do it. At least I think he is. Maybe not, I don't know.

Take La Bessoune, now, they say she was having a secret love affair and she never told nobody about it, and it drove her crazy. She couldn't call it off, see, it was stronger than she was. So was she free? There's them as says it was the devil made her do it, and others says it was the priest, but whatever it was she couldn't find no other way out, poor woman. The Good Lord must have had mercy on her, because she died with his medals around her neck.

Sometimes it ain't easy to feel sorry for your sins. You try your best, you argue with yourself, you try to make yourself do what's right, you bang your thick skull against all your firm intentions, but you just can't get them into your heart. Sometimes a person just ain't free to feel regret for what she's doing.

Just before it gets dark, when the sea changes colour and the gulls all start their screeching, I sometimes go for a walk on the bridge, and I wait. I wait to see if a steamer reappears that went down outside the bay during the war, the last war, with all souls on board. And I remember the song he used to sing, sitting by himself in the bow, apart from the others. He had yellow hair and big troubled eyes, and if the war hadn't taken him, if he'd of asked me to go away with him, somewhere far off, into a foreign country, to leave Gapi and the kids, if . . . but he didn't ask me and I stayed on here. Who knows ahead of time what a person would do if she had it to do all over, eh? Anyways, you don't get to do it all over again. Which is why I don't see why we got to go to so much trouble coming up ahead of time with them firm intentions.

Especially when it ain't all that sure we're ever going to need them.

If only we could know. To be sure before we got to the Other Side. Once we're there, of course, it'll be too late. Whatever we've done, we've done. If there ain't nothing on the Other Side then we wouldn't need to waste a lot of time worrying about it on this side. We could live out the time that's given to us. It may not be a lot, but we could spend it without all them knots in our stomachs. And if there is something there, what'd it be, do you think? What the Christ, do you think we'll have to start our suffering all over again? Ain't we had enough of that? Will we have to go through more of it, through all the eternity the Good Lord gives us, freezing our asses off from the beginning of Advent to the end of Lent, eating warmed-over beans from one Sunday to the next, selling clams and mussels and quahogs door to door, wearing the doctor's wife's clothes they gave you out of charity, burying your children before they're even old enough to get their eyes open? Jesus, do you think it's possible?

It ain't like we asked for much. We didn't even ask to be born, if you want to look at it that way. And we sure don't ask to die, neither. And you think they're going to hand us another life on the Other Side that's the same as this one here? Except that one we won't have the freedom to turn down, there's no way we'll be able to get out of it. Gapi, he says we can always go down and throw ourselves off the dock when we've had enough of this vale of tears, but is there going to be a dock on the Other Side?

I think maybe I'll go and see that doctor after all.

A little peace and quiet on this side, that's all I ask. I won't sin no more, I promise. There comes a time in a person's life when she ain't got the taste or the energy for sinning anyways. They want me to go to mass and the sacraments, fine, I'll go. They want me to go to vespers for the whole of their eternity, forever and ever amen, I'm there. Whatever it takes. I'll be on my best behaviour and be as sorry as I can be if I offend you in the tiniest way. But let that be the end on it. No more freezing cold winters, no more baked beans, no more pain in the guts. Let's call 'er quits.

Of course, if things is better on the Other Side we ain't going to look a gift horse in the mouth. We ain't used to asking for such things, is all. We don't ask for castles in California or plastic flowers. But if from time to time the angels saw fit to serve us up some duck stew and store-bought coconut pie, and if God the Father in the flesh felt like calling the square dance on a Saturday night, we wouldn't want to disappoint them. If that's what Paradise is like then we wouldn't balk no more at death . . . we wouldn't be afraid to die . . . we'd welcome death with open arms, God knows we would!

As it is, I'm going to go see that doctor. First thing tomorrow.

Ever since *La Sagouine* gave Acadian culture a popular voice more than thirty years ago, Antonine Maillet's sparkling imagination, her wry and wildly inventive writing, and her versatility have been recognized at home and abroad. Writing for both adults and children, she is the author of many novels, story collections, and plays, as well as numerous radio and television scripts. For her Homeric novel *Pélagie-la-Charette*, she became the first non-citizen of France to receive the prestigious Prix Goncourt, and she won a Governor General's Award for *Don l'Orignal*, her fable about the creation of Acadie. Maillet divides her time between her birthplace, Bouctouche, New Brunswick, and Montreal.

Wayne Grady is the author of ten books of non-fiction, the translator of ten more books, and the editor of six literary anthologies. One of Canada's most distinguished literary translators, he won the John Glassco Prize for *Christopher Cartier of Hazelnut* by Antonine Maillet, and the Governor General's Award for *On the Eighth Day*, his rollicking translation of Maillet's novel *Le Huitième Jour*.